Murder
In the Rockies

The Ghost & the Camper Kooky Mystery Series

Book 4

Rita Moreau

Murder In the Rockies
Copyright © 2022 Rita Moreau

Cover art by LLewellenDesigns.com
Formatting by Jesse Gordon

Printed in the United States of America

Titles by Rita Moreau

Mary Catherine Mahoney Series
Novels
Bribing Saint Anthony
Nuns! Psychics! & Gypsies! OH NO!!
Feisty Nuns
The House on Xenia
Novella
The Russian & Aunt Sophia
The Ghost & the Camper Series
Novels
Wheeler-Dealer
Murder on Honky-Tonk Row
Murder in the Badlands

This book is dedicated to my husband George, the love of my life, and, as he loved to tell everyone, "I'm the author's husband." I promise to honor the essence of your rich life by following your lead. Live life to the fullest, do it your way, but don't forget to have fun. I am what I am because you loved me. Until we meet again, my love.

The Rockies
Chapter 1

I stepped out of my Airstream, holding a warm cup of coffee. Still, in my Minnie Mouse pajamas and robe, I peeked around the campground to make sure no one else was stirring.

I took a breath of cool air and looked up at one of the most famous landmarks in the country, Mount Rushmore. It was a few days after the 4th of July—and I knew by mid-day it would be a scorcher.

I sat down under the awning of my camper, tucked between two Airstreams. I never tire of looking at them. We had been a group of four Airstreams—back at the beginning of this adventure. Along the way, we lost one that had belonged to a wheeler-dealer, but that's another story.

Right now, there were the three of us. Parked in a row, they looked like three shiny toasters lined up on the counter of a diner. To the right was Lili and Bob Young's 27 ft. Airstream. Their model is called a Flying Cloud. It has a unique feature: a rear hatch that you can open for the ultimate view at dinner or let the breeze flow through. Loading and unloading gear was a piece of cake for them. They tow their Airstream with a red F-150. Lili picked out the color.

Usually, Bob would be the first one up. He likes to take an early morning ride on his Harley. Guess it reminds him of when he started in the Los Angeles Police Department and rode a motorcycle—before he worked his way up to a homicide detective. Lili is ever organized when she wakes up and has something ready to bake. Like her tasty buttermilk biscuits or cinnamon coffee cake.

I found myself the early bird this morning as I sat drinking my coffee in the pre-dawn light. It had been an exhilarating but exhausting couple of days. Not only had we celebrated the 4th of July at Mount Rushmore, with all the fireworks, but once again, we found ourselves smack dab in the middle of a mystery. A Marine buddy of Bob's asked him to investigate the death of his son, whose death had been ruled an accident. It turned out to be murder.

Lili and I have been best friends for a long time. Following my divorce, Lili invited me to travel with them over the summer months in their Airstream.

"It's time, Mabel. Shake those hips your Mama gave you," as Lili aptly put it, and then did a shake, rattle, and roll with her Rubenesque hips so I would get her point.

I gave it a lot of thought and even more brainstorming with Lili and Bob. I didn't want to be the third wheel all summer; I was so tired of that—so I took a leap of faith and, with Bob's help, I went shopping, and the next thing I knew, I was the proud owner of a vintage Airstream. The model is called a Caravel and is light enough to be towed with an SUV. When I found out it was simple to maneuver and easy to fit into a small campground spot, I pulled out my checkbook. The comforts of home were not missing because it was refurbished from top to bottom. Bob suggested something with more muscle than an SUV, so I'm towing my Airstream with a *Men in Black* F-150. Lili helped me find the courage to take my life back. I'm now RV'ing all the way from Florida to the Wild Wild West.

I turned to look at the Airstream on my left. It belonged to the Crawfords—Josh and Peggy—retired schoolteachers. They had a "Do Not Disturb" sign on the door to their camper. Their Airstream was a 22-ft. Caravel. They were towing it with an SUV, a dark blue Suburban which was as big as our trucks. I could hear their a/c running. They keep it at a temperature colder than a meat locker.

I sipped my coffee and thought about how far I had come—literally and figuratively. Two thousand miles, numerous campgrounds, and lots of excitement along the way.

My name is Mabel Gold. I assumed when I got to the seventh decade of my life, I'd be doing a lot of baking and entertaining grandchildren. Nope. Instead, here I was—driving an F-150, towing a vintage Airstream camper, and doing it all by myself.

For a while there, I was a wreck—too many Cosmos, too much junk food—and all because I couldn't figure out what the fondue happened. After forty years of what I thought was a happy marriage and five—yes, five — kids, my husband Jack lost his marbles, which were already loose, and fell for Tiffanie. She's about the same age as Bianca, our (millennial) daughter.

Unfortunately for Jack, Tiffanie didn't take to motherhood. Nor was being married to a rich plastic surgeon enough for her. It looks like she's going to take him to the cleaners. They have split, and meanwhile, he has taken custody of their twin boys, and now Jack is getting hands-on experience changing diapers—karma.

Today we're leaving Mount Rushmore and the Badlands for the largest mountain range west of the Mississippi, the Rocky Mountains. It's about a 6-to-7-hour drive for a caravan of three Airstreams till we reach our next campground in Estes Park, Colorado. I know when we get there, and I look at towering mountains that disappear into the clouds, it will bring tears to my eyes. Doesn't matter if it's the 1st or the 100th time you see the Rocky Mountains—the tears will flow.

My five kids thought I lost some of the pieces of my puzzle back when I picked up and left Long Island and moved to Florida. Buying a vintage Airstream with a snazzy pickup truck convinced them I had not only lost my puzzle pieces, but they were all over the floor.

I won't tell them, but they could be right because I discovered my Airstream came with something extra: a ghost, a spirit, a specter, whatever you want to call her. Her name is Irma, and she's been dead for a stretch. Not only that, but I can also see her and talk to her, or maybe it was the other way around because she's chatty and bossy to boot.

Seems Irma was a showgirl in Vegas and later a madam of what polite folks call a cat house. She's been handed a long sentence in purgatory. I didn't ask why. Don't need to know those details. She periodically checks in with Saint Peter.

"He reminds me of my parole officer," Irma told me when we first met, and then she proceeded to tell me that my role would be to help her get out of purgatory. Seems she's been stuck there for quite some time. But the good news is that every time Irma does a good deed on earth, it brings her closer to the pearly gates and out the front door of my camper.

"The best good deed, Mabel, is solving a murder. Double murders are even better. Two for the price of one. And Mabel, do your best to avoid stumbling over bodies."

I reluctantly agreed to help her. What choice did I have?

Irma did move a couple notches closer to heaven when we solved murders in Savannah, Nashville, and one that took place at Mount Rushmore. But the last time I checked, she's still here.

As I drank my coffee, I saw the first rays of sunshine peeking out between the ponderosa pine trees, and I could hear the birds starting to chirp. I reflected on my journey—not only in my camper but in my life since it took an unexpected detour.

I was at a fork in the road—a mighty big one—it took up most of the road. Irma, who I've warmed up to, is right there with me. She's between her prior life and the gates of heaven. Me—I'm between my old life and who the crepe suzette knows? At some point, I'll need to grab that fork and move on. In the meantime, I'll be camping, buckled up and ready for the ride. Are you coming? Hope you like camping.

Chapter 2

I finished my coffee, went inside, changed out of my Minnie Mouse PJs, and came back out to tackle my chores to get ready to leave the campground. Bob was up and doing the same as was Josh. Bob always offered to help me, but I knew I needed to do it myself. Like I have since I found out about Jack and the gold digger he was spending a little too much time with.

I have several checklists to make sure I forgot nothing, so I would be cleared for takeoff. I have a departure checklist, which covers the interior and the exterior. Everything needs to be latched and secured for the interior and disconnected and stowed for the exterior. I don't want to be picking up broken dishes or last night's leftovers off the floor when we arrive at our next campground or must stop on the road to close the awning, which came loose and was flapping in the wind because I forgot to secure the travel latch. Nor do I relish draining the black tank (yes, it's called black for a reason), but after spilling the hose a few times (yuck), I made sure I was carefully unhooking the hose, and I never ever run out of plastic gloves.

Everything on my list was there for a reason, and that reason was I had forgotten to do it, or I did it the wrong way. Story of my life at the current juncture.

The newest item on my checklist was to secure Toto's cage. He's my emotional support pet. A prairie dog. I didn't even know that they could be pets, but he was given to me while we were in the Badlands, and so now, he's one more item to check off before takeoff.

I made sure I cuddled him a little before I secured his cage and added some fresh grass. Prairie dogs need affection.

Bob did a last walk around all three Airstreams. When he gave us a thumbs up, we pulled out of the campground in a uniform order—like a marching band in Macy's parade. We usually drew a crowd when we left. I saluted Mount Rushmore one more time, and before I knew it, we were heading south on the road that would lead us to the Rocky Mountains. We were a sight to see, three Airstreams as shiny as a mirror with that iconic Airstream curved aluminum design. It's a design like no other RV on the road and one that turns heads wherever we go. Sometimes called the Silver Bullet, I even found out you can drive it a short distance with a flat tire.

Driving behind the wheel of Thor, my nickname for my F-150, I always feel like pinching myself. And thanks to Lili's twin sister Jolene, my truck is emblazoned with Thor's name in gold lettering on both sides. Who knew Jolene had artistic talent besides knowing how to shoot a gun?

Once we were on the highway, Irma materialized. She rides shotgun in my F-150. From time to time, she threatens to take the wheel.

"Mabel, remember I told you that when I was on parole, I drove an 18-wheeler? A Peterbilt, by the way."

Today Irma appeared in her Annie Oakley outfit. I never knew what to expect. With a jam-packed closet in ghostly cyberspace, Irma can switch from one outfit to another faster than you can snap your fingers and chew bubble gum at the same time. Tall and slim with movie star looks and shimmering auburn hair, I looked over at a cowgirl hat, denim dress with fringe, lots of fringe, and cowgirl boots with red, white, and blue beads, lots of beads. The 4th of July had just passed.

I must admit, I enjoy Irma's company as we travel across the country. It's good to have someone to talk to about life, even if that someone is dead. She's become a friend, a genuine friend. Not like the ones I thought were friends back in Long Island who dropped me as soon as the ink was dry on my divorce papers, and I was no longer a member of their swanky country club. Of course, I'm not telling Irma that. Her head is already big enough.

In her living days, Irma was a showgirl and then a madam of a high-class bordello run by the mob in Las Vegas. They liked her because she was bossy, and trust me, she still is. They also liked that she was an expert judge of people and could manage her girls. Irma told me my Airstream came with a name—Betsy after her sister who adopted her son at birth and waits patiently for her at the pearly gates.

When Irma talks about Betsy, her voice softens, and her eyes close. Sometimes tears appear, which she quickly wipes away with a swirl of her ghostly hand.

She watched her son, Walt, grow up from afar. The night her life came to an end was when she took a bullet to save her son right outside my Airstream. That was also when she met her son. As she lay dying in his arms, he asked her what her name was, and she told him—Mom. Some memories never die and live on, even after death.

I mentioned that I have five kids. And I'm really proud of them. Daughter number one, my oldest, is Margaret. I like to call her Meg, but she doesn't like that. She prefers Margaret. She's a lawyer, a good one, the kind you need if you know where the bodies are buried. About the time daughter number one started suggesting I consider moving into an old folk's home, which she calls an active older adult community, I decided to move to Florida. I wanted to get away from Long Island, where everybody knew my name and my sad story.

A lot of those same people live in those active older adult communities. They have cheery names like "Sunset Village" or "Autumn Wind" in the colorful brochures Margaret discreetly left for me when she came by to visit. I had to look. They all showed good-looking seniors—that's what the brochures dubbed people my age—attractive and fit, playing golf or tennis with big smiles plastered on their faces. Me? I have a hard time reaching down for my car keys, let alone a tennis ball. Playing golf would put me in traction.

Margaret hasn't given up because she plans to show me some of those *senior homes* in person when, as she put it, "You've finished your little summer camping trip and are back in Florida for the winter."

I should have reminded Margaret that at the end of my little summer camping trip, I would have driven a truck and towed a camper over four thousand miles all by myself! How's that for an active older adult?

Besides Margaret, I have two other daughters, Cecilia and Bianca. Cecilia took a break from her dream of seeing her name in lights on a marquee on Broadway and came to visit me when we were camping in Nashville. That's when she found the love of her life, Joe, an aspiring country music singer who had joined us on our first stop in Savannah. She and Joe are now married and expecting. No time to waste. Cecilia's biological clock was loudly ticking. Unlike her younger sister Bianca, she prefers to bring children into the world traditionally, marriage and then children.

Bianca, the youngest of my daughters, has her own ideas. Fiercely independent, she took her love of baking to a new level when she became an award-winning pastry chef.

She started a pop-up bakery featuring cupcakes. It's now a successful and thriving business. Bianca wasn't waiting for her "prince charming," and without batting an eye, she told me, "When the time comes to have a baby, I'll have a baby."

I sometimes wonder if there was a mix-up at the hospital when Bianca was born. Lately, she's been dropping hints in her texts that she might come to visit, which has me wondering why. That daughter never makes a move without a business plan.

My son Henry works alongside Bianca in the cupcake factory and teaches yoga. He's gay and came to visit recently when we were in the Badlands. He brought along his love, Barry, a student he met in his yoga class. I adore Henry. He's my closest confidante—as I am his. We talk or text almost daily. I knew he was gay early on. When it was time to have a talk with Jack, he called me, and I could hear the tremble in his voice.

"What did he say?"

"Dad just said he was wondering when I was going to get around to telling him and then took me out for a drink. We went to a gay bar, and he met a lot of my friends."

Jack was a decent father; I'll give him that.

My oldest son, Jack Jr., is a financial planner. Jack had wanted him to go to medical school and join him in his medical practice. Turned out Jack Jr. was squeamish about blood, but he did love numbers. And money. So, he went his own way and became a financial doctor. With his handsome good looks—like his father—and a silver tongue, he is very successful.

Which, of course, makes his wife Carmela happy. She loves money, too. He makes it, and she spends it. But not on food. She is pencil thin. Wears a size zero or something like that. I never liked her, and she likes me even less. She drops hints about my weight when I visit.

"Oh, Mabel, let me set you up with my trainer. He's a former Seal—he'll get you in shape in no time."

Yikes! I could just see myself lifting a log on my shoulder! So, what if I've got a few extra pounds, and she looks like a runway model?

It doesn't help that Carmela is a superb cook and always makes fantastic meals when I visit. She sits there during dinner and picks at her food and drinks way too much wine while I scarf down chocolate pie with whipped cream. All I can say is wait till she goes through menopause. Meanwhile, I play nicey-nicey, so I can visit my two granddaughters.

* * *

Lili's husband, Bob, is the leader of our little group. The caravan idea had been his from the beginning. His experience in the Special Forces and the LAPD made us all feel comfortable taking on this adventure.

He takes great care to navigate our route to accommodate three Airstreams towed by pickup trucks and an SUV. Before we left Florida, Bob poured over maps and created an Excel spreadsheet of all our destinations and campgrounds and the sights we were going to see along the way. Marines plan ahead!

"We want to avoid mountainous roads that can become crooked and narrow, making passing difficult. These are called "switchback roads," many with "hairpin" turns. Some of those roads don't have guardrails," Bob told us before we left the Badlands.

"What do you mean the roads don't have guardrails?" I asked.

"Guardrails, meaning if you overreach the bend in

that hairpin turn, you and your Airstream go headfirst over the side of a mountain, and it's a long way down."

"Oh," I said, with that picture forever stamped in my mind.

"We will be camped near the Rocky Mountain National Park. It has the most paved roads of any national park, and I plan to ride my Harley on as many of those roads as I can and take a selfie at the Continental Divide," Bob said with a big smile.

Lili and I added our own points of interest to Bob's list. One was the Stanley Hotel—the hotel in Estes Park, which inspired Stephen King to write the novel that became Stanley Kubrick's 1980 classic cult film "The Shining."

Lili and I had watched "The Shining" before we left Boca Vista. As far as I was concerned, it was right up there with the Exorcist. What surprised me was that Irma had no desire whatsoever to visit the Stanley Hotel. Which was odd since she has never missed an opportunity to tag along wherever I go.

"What's up with you, Irma? Don't you want to check it out and meet other peeps on your side of the fence?"

"No, thank you, Mabel, and that's all I have to say about that Stanley Hotel."

Several hours into our trip, we made a stop at a visitor's center that offered parking for campers and gave us a break to stretch our legs. Peggy, our resident schoolteacher, grabbed some brochures at the visitor's center and commenced a history lesson about nearby Custer State Park.

"State parks are as beautiful as our national parks

and should not be overlooked," Peggy said as she scanned us to make sure we were paying attention.

"Custer State Park encompasses 71,000 acres in the Black Hills. The granite peaks and rolling plains are calling. The clear mountain waters are inviting, and the open ranges are waiting to be discovered. Come to Custer State Park and let yourself run wild."

I snuck a look at Lili and rolled my eyeballs—the last thing I wanted to see was Peggy running wild.

Peggy's hair was cropped short, and it was gray. She didn't bother with coloring it. She wore almond-shaped cat glasses, retro and coming back in style. I think hers are original. They remind me of what our school librarian wore when I was in grade school.

Josh, her husband, was Peggy's shadow. He said little because Peggy did enough talking for both of them. He had taught American history.

He looked like a history professor, with his horn-rimmed glasses and disheveled hair. He was usually dressed in khaki shorts and boat shoes. If you squinted your eyes, he had a ruggedly handsome look—he had an Indiana Jones vibe.

As of late, Lili and I have started to notice a change in Josh. First, he was drinking a tad more than he usually did when we gathered for our evening happy hour. Next, he was becoming more sociable, a new side we had not seen up to this point in our trip. It was like a caterpillar becoming a butterfly. As he loosened up, we found he was also likable and actually had a witty sense of humor. We could tell this was new to Peggy, who wasn't comfortable socializing.

"She doesn't know how to socialize," Lili said. "She never had to as a school principal."

"I guess not," I responded. "She ran the joint."

Peggy appeared to welcome this new dynamic growing between the two of them. They started holding hands when they took walks. She blushed when Josh winked at her, and now, she was adding jokes to her lessons. She knew a lot of jokes, as it turned out.

"I think Peggy could make a darn good standup comedian," I said to Lili after one of her jokes left us laughing for the rest of the day.

"Maybe we should take Peggy to a comedy club when we get to Colorado," Lili said with a grin.

"Maybe we should," I said. "Peggy might even get up there and do a comedy routine. Find a second career."

A few days before we left the Badlands, Peggy, drinking a little more wine than usual, confided to Lili and me that she and Josh were on this trip to bring the spark back into their marriage.

"Josh and I've been married a long time. Our kids are all grown and moved away with lives of their own. When we retired, we realized it was more spouse time and less money. Neither one of us had anything to retire to."

She then paused and looked around to make sure nobody was nearby and could overhear what she was about to say. I held my breath. Not sure I wanted to hear anything about issues in their marriage, especially if it involved their bedroom. I was about to suggest brushing up on a comedy act when she added, "I'd like to investigate getting contacts and changing the color of my hair. Can you help me?"

"Sure," I said with obvious relief in my voice. Thank goodness we weren't going into their bedroom. Changing hair color and getting contacts was something I could handle.

"What color would you like your hair to be?"

"I'd like to be a blonde—you know, like Marilyn was."

Peggy was softening. Finally, letting go of being a school principal.

"Well, this is interesting," Peggy said as she continued her history lesson on Custer State Park. "In 1988, the Galena Fire, started by lightning, burned 16,002 acres."

She looked up from what she was reading and remarked, "Did you know Galena is also the name of the main ore in lead? It's such a grand word. I wonder if anyone ever names their baby Galena?"

I bit my tongue in order not to say, "Who in the world would name their baby after the main ore in lead?" Even a geologist wouldn't go there. Although on second thought, I wouldn't be surprised if my daughter Bianca would name her children after the names of rocks. Was I going to have future grandchildren whose names were granite or marble? I returned my mind to the classroom on that note.

Peggy continued, "In 1990, the Cicero Peak Fire, started by a spark from logging equipment outside of the park, burned 4,510 acres in the park and 14,203 total. In 2017, the Legion Lake Fire was one of the largest wildfires in South Dakota history. It burned 54,000 acres."

"Were any buffalo killed?" Lili wanted to know.

I gave Lili you-know-the-rules look—NO QUES-TIONS—or we'd be in history class all day, but Lili had a special spot in her heart for living creatures, even bugs except palmetto bugs. That's where she drew the line. So, do I.

When I moved to Florida, I discovered one evening what a palmetto bug looked like when I was watching TV, and something caught the corner of my eye. I looked up, and there was a bug that had survived three hundred million years crawling across my ceiling. I ran and got my broom and tried to swat it off my ceiling, and that's when I learned they could fly, and they tend to fly toward shadows, meaning you. Once it landed on the floor, I also found out the hard way you don't want to step on these ancient survivors. They don't squish well. Very scary bugs.

"It doesn't mention anything about buffalos. Good question, Lili," the schoolmarm said.

"Peggy, where did the name Rocky Mountains come from?" I asked. What the heck? Lili now mirrored the same look I had just given her. Peggy was a great teacher. Plus, it was quicker to ask Peggy than Alexa. Whenever we needed to know something, even Bob would say, "Let's go ask Peggy."

Peggy paused and looked at Josh, who picked up the history lesson. After all, that was his element.

"Indigenous peoples inhabited the prairies east of the Rocky Mountains. From the prairies, they could see a large rocky mass which they called "*as-sin-wati*." Translated, this means Rocky Mountains."

While we were in the Badlands, Josh displayed a special interest in Native Americans, or, as he called them, indigenous people. He explained indigenous peoples are distinct social and cultural groups that share collective ancestral ties to the lands and natural resources where they live, occupy, or from which they have been displaced.

Peggy gave Josh a broad smile, which he returned with a playful wink. This brought a hint of pink to Peggy's cheeks. A real blush—not one from the make-up counter. We hadn't gotten that far yet, as Peggy only recently discovered the cost of cosmetics. If she thought that was a cultural shock, I wondered what she would think when she realized the cost involved in coloring your hair.

Irma chose this time to pop in and whisper in my ear, "Did you know buffalo can mate with a cow?"

"Ugh!" I whispered as she smiled sheepishly.

She smirked and took off as Bob walked over to tell us it was time to get back on the road. I was happy to get going and just hoped that Irma would stay away for a while and not try to give me a biology lesson.

Chapter 3

As we continued our trip from the Badlands to the Rockies, Irma sang John Denver's tune, *Rocky Mountain High*, to make sure I kept my eyes on the road. I wasn't falling asleep. I just couldn't stop looking at the amazing view. We would come around a bend, and a gigantic mountain would appear along with enormous boulders lining the side of the road. I loved John Denver and sang along. Even my bobblehead Groot danced on my dashboard.

Irma stopped singing. I decided it might be a good thing to chat while I kept my eyes on the road.

"You know, Irma, one of the main reasons I bought this Airstream was because it was refurbished from top to bottom."

"Yes. And I must say I didn't appreciate being stuck for three months in the factory while they were doing the work. It was very noisy."

I kept my eye on Bob. I kept a certain distance between Bob and me, just as Josh kept a certain distance between him and me. We never wanted to leave a gap where cars would cut in between us. I kept talking to Annie Oakley.

"Another reason, Irma, was Airstreams are easy to tow—of course, the F-150 I bought to tow it helps."

"Maybe you should have bought one that parked itself," Irma said sarcastically.

I didn't really have any problem parking. Bob made sure of that before we left Fish Camp. We practiced for weeks in an empty parking lot. But he did try to make it easy on all of us by always booking a pull-through campsite. That's a campsite that has both an entrance and an exit, so you can easily pull into the spot to park and then drive straight through it when you are ready to leave.

"Airstream is working on that. The other day, Sid texted that Airstream has a new prototype that will park itself."

"Mabel, you're lucky to have such a smart grandson and sweet to boot," Irma said.

That brought a smile to my face. My grandson Sid and I are very close.

"I sure am. And he keeps me updated on everything electronic. He just told me that Airstream is testing an electric travel trailer that will be able to go off-grid for weeks at a time, park itself into a camping spot, and help propel itself down the road. It's called the eStream, and it will be the first electric-powered camper in the United States."

"Wow! That sounds special. How much is it?" Irma asked.

"Don't know, but a new Airstream goes for over $100,000.

"You might want to start saving your pennies."

"Since the eStream won't be available for a while. I'll have time to do that. But, what with inflation, it should probably be quarters."

"Right. Geez, I remember when the price of a gallon of gas jumped to a dollar in the 1970s, and everybody panicked. Waiting in line for gas around the block for hours."

A reminder that Irma had lived in a different time zone. She was born in 1948 and died in 1998.

"Sid was so excited when I bought Betsy. He called to tell me all about the history of Airstreams."

The mention of her sister's name always brought a smile to Irma's face.

"Airstreams have a long history. They're still hand-made to order in the Airstream factory in Ohio. Sporting the same silver aluminum body as it did in the 1930s. Plus, each unit contains between 4,000 and 7,000 rivets, and the cabinetry is custom made."

Before I knew it, Irma was dressed like Rosie the Riveter. She now wore a red and white polka dot bandana and a dark blue work shirt and jeans. She kept her red, white, and blue beaded boots.

"Rosie the Riveter wore a bandana because women working in factories during World War II wore bandanas to keep their hair out of the machines and equipment they used."

As I got to know Irma, I found myself learning a lot from my ghostly sidekick.

"As a showgirl in Vegas, you met members of the mob all the time. In fact, that's how I came to run one of their cat houses. They approached me to take over as head madam of the house. They knew I had management skills since I worked my way up to head showgirl at the casino where they had an ownership interest," Irma told me shortly after we first met.

Irma flexed her bicep like Rosie the Riveter and smiled.

"You know Irma, Sid even told me how you can tell if an Airstream is vintage or not."

"Do tell."

"You have to check out the last set of numbers on the VIN. If you see a set of four numbers, this puts your Airstream in the 70s. If you see a set of three numbers, your Airstream is a 60s model."

"Your grandson is so smart," Irma said wistfully. "I sure hope that one day I can see my grandchildren. I keep wondering about them."

I knew from our chats that her son Walt lived in Wyoming and had several children.

"Irma, it's funny, but I'm seeing more of my kids on this road trip than if I'd stayed home in Boca Vista."

"Roger that," Irma said.

I glanced at her. Then I asked Irma a question that had been on my mind. "Irma, if I bought a newer Airstream—and you're still in purgatory—would you come along with me?"

"Nope." Irma looked straight ahead. "Can't."

Right then and there, I decided I would never trade

Betsy for a newer model, even if it could park itself and cook a gourmet meal.

"Well, that settles it. I'm not trading in Betsy. I'll just have Sid drive us when the time comes. I mean, if you're still around."

With that, Irma reached over and put her ghostly hand on mine. It felt strange, like a gentle cool breeze.

Chapter 4

Later in the afternoon, we arrived at the campground in Estes Park. At 8,000 plus feet, our campground was surrounded by the majestic Rocky Mountains. There were many campers, from big rig RV'ers to minimalist tent-dwellers.

We came to a stop in front of the campground office. As usual, Bob took care of our check-in. When he came out of the campground office carrying a map of the campground, he was followed by a man who looked like a hippie with his long white hair pulled back in a braided ponytail. Pushing eighty. With his well-worn Hawaiian shirt, baggy shorts, black socks, and white sneakers, he looked a lot like someone I'd see in the aisles at a grocery store back in Florida. He was smoking a pipe.

Later, after we had set up our Airstreams, reversing what I did when we left the Badlands in the morning. I asked Bob about the campground manager.

"His name is Al. He's a nice old coot and even told me where I could get some fly-fishing lessons. I'm going to check it out in the morning."

"Bob, was Al smoking weed in that pipe of his?"

"He sure was."

"Does that bother you?"

Bob shook his head and smiled. "No, Mabel, not a bit. It's legal in the state of Colorado. No one's breaking the law here."

Once we were settled, we reconvened for happy hour outside Bob and Lili's Airstream, which had become a tradition on the trip. Some nights we met for a drink and then took off to see local sites and try local cuisine. Other nights we stayed put, fired up the grill, and sat around the fire pit for hours. But after our long trip, we all decided to have an early night.

Josh and Peggy dropped by to say hello and then excused themselves to take a walk around the campground, holding hands.

Lili suggested that since Bob was going fishing in the morning, she and I should take a trip into town. Perhaps stop by a casino and then go out to lunch and do a little shopping. Bob said he was going to ask Josh to join him for the fly-fishing lesson. I glanced at Lili, and I could see we both had the same idea. Hopefully, Peggy would tag along with the guys.

She might want to learn about fly-fishing. Or give lectures about it.

Lili and I intended to enjoy the air of a casino. I love to play the penny slots, and Lili was going to use some of her skills just for fun. Her twin, Jolene, had put the bug in her ear when she joined us in the Badlands to solve the murder of the son of Bob's Marine buddy. Lili has never shared with me exactly what her twin does, but it was apparently so hush-hush that Jolene would probably have to shoot you if you found out.

I whispered to Lili, "We're going to have fun, but don't be surprised if Irma shows up. She has a new friend she wants us to meet."

Of course, Lili knew all about Irma.

After all, when Irma first showed up, I thought I might actually be going ga-ga. Just to make sure I wasn't the only one ready for the funny farm, I had to tell someone. It sure wasn't going to be one of my five kids. It turned out that after a little practice and the help of reading glasses she hadn't worn since her cataract surgery, Lili could see Irma. It probably came from the fact that Lili grew up in New Orleans and—like me— saw ghosts as a kid. Somewhere along the line back in Brooklyn, I had lost the talent, but when it came back, it came back in full force—or should I say like Ghost Busters!

Of course, Bob knew about Irma. Lili couldn't keep a secret from him. And although he was skeptical, he was able to approach it with an open attitude. He explained it to me.

"Look, Mabel, my attitude is that anything is possible. As a Marine and a homicide detective, I've seen my share of miracles. But I've also witnessed too many deaths. More than once, I've felt something. A wisp of chilly air. A spark of light. I have just always thought of it as a guardian angel showing up."

I felt so lucky that the Youngs were in my life. They are just great people. Bob and Lili are an example of opposites attracting. They are a perfectly matched couple like salt and pepper. Bob, 70ish, is white and conservative. Lili, a few years younger, is ebony and a feisty activist. They had known each other for years and only got together after Lili's husband, Carl, died because of his bravery as an NYFD first responder during 9/11. He had rushed in and up the stairs of North Tower. He survived, but his lungs never recovered. When he passed away, Bob attended Carl's funeral.

"Carl and Bob had been friends since they went through basic training as Marines," explained Lili. "After the funeral, Bob stayed in touch through all the hard years I was working as a housekeeper on Long Island. He would check up on me. Make sure I was okay. When he got divorced, he came a calling. And I answered."

That's where I met Lili. On Long Island, where I had a big, fancy house. Not as big as the ones where Lili worked as a head housekeeper. She worked for the Downton Abbey wannabees.

For some reason, Lili and I hit it off. Perhaps because I was never one of those country club types. I preferred playing with my kids rather than playing with tennis pros. We connected over a school play where she was chaperoning and cheering on a rich kid—the daughter of a famous couple who didn't have time to do their own cheering.

Over the years, we got to know each other. I discovered that she was considered the best in the business, and couples tried to steal her to work in their megamansions because she was known for her discretion as much as for her organizational skills. Unlike so many estate managers, Lili never blabbed. She would take her employer's secrets to the grave. Not to the paparazzi.

One of the reasons for her success was that the people she hired were equally qualified and loyal. This was not by accident. She put applicants through a vigorous vetting—over a game of poker. If they could beat her at poker, she wouldn't hire them.

When she told me the story, I was shocked. "Gee, Lili, that doesn't seem fair."

"Mabel, to be a good poker player, you have to have skills—and being able to lie with a straight face is high on the list. My father used the same test.

"He loved to play cards, but he knew the danger of the gambling muse. For him, it was just for fun, and he loved teaching me and Jolene. But my sister never was interested. But he would take me along with him sometimes to our local social club. I'm not sure if it was to distract the other players or because he realized I could count cards. But I loved it because I got to spend time with him."

"So why didn't you become a professional and play on the poker circuit?"

"I gave it some serious thought, but one night I met a young man by the name of Carl, and the rest is history."

Chapter 5

The next morning, we woke up feeling refreshed. The air was clear, and the sun was rising on the horizon. After the long drive, we had called it an early night.

While Peggy and I were sipping our coffee and nibbling on blueberry muffins, we watched as Bob and Josh pulled out their fishing gear. Peggy was wearing a red and green lumberjack shirt. And so was Josh.

"You and Josh look ready for fishing with those matching shirts."

"Aren't they cute? Josh bought them as a surprise. I'm not going to fish, but I will take lots of photos. Are you sure you and Lili don't want to join us?"

"Too fishy for me. But I will eat whatever the guys catch. Fish is high up there on my diet."

According to Peggy, there are only a handful of casinos in Colorado, and they were about an hour away from our campground. Peggy told me this when I asked her where the nearest casino was. Not only was asking Peggy quicker than googling, but she sometimes was more up-to-date than our devices.

to get a good look at this new apparition and then looked back at me.

"Hello, ladies. So nice to finally meet you. Irma has told me all about you."

As best as I could, without running off the road, I kept staring at Ted. He looked so much like someone we both knew back in Florida. His name is Limo Louie. He's a lawyer who works out of the back of his limousine, yes, like the Lincoln lawyer. When he's a little short on cash, he uses his limo to Uber and Door Dash. Hence the nickname. We are friends, but if he had it his way, we'd be more than friends.

I kept sneaking peeks. Ted was better looking—darn good looking, for that matter. Ted looked tall. It appeared as if he had long legs stretched out before him. He also had a voice. What some would call a radio voice. Rich and deep, with a tone of authority and leadership. I couldn't keep my eyes off him and kept sneaking peeks.

Ted flashed me a million-dollar smile. Oh boy, this man was going to be trouble. Dead or alive.

Chapter 6

I glanced again at Ted, who smiled and gave me a wink. I felt myself blush.

"Mabel, how about if we pull over and have a chat? You and Lili can stretch your legs, and perhaps Irma will take the opportunity to pop into her bottomless closet."

"Okay. Good idea."

It was weird to follow the commands of a ghost, but he had that effect on me. He probably had the same effect when he was alive.

I drove a few more miles until we came to a spot where it would be safe to pull off the road. It was a pretty spot under a tree with a view of the mountains.

"Let's get out and talk," Ted said.

By the time I unbuckled my seat belt Ted was standing beside my door like a gentleman. As Lili and I hopped out of Thor, I saw I was right. Ted was tall.

I looked around. There was not a soul around—well, other than the two living and two dead. Ted was wearing a bomber jacket, a classic safari shirt, and a pair of army air corps officer trousers. He topped it off with a fedora, which he took off and tipped our way. I could see he had a headful of thick hair, dark and curly, with just a hint of gray on his sideburns.

Standing next to him was Irma. She, too, had taken his suggestion. She was now wearing her Mata Hari spy outfit. I recognized it from the old movie with Greta Garbo.

Ted smiled. I don't know if it was at Irma's outfit or if it was for me.

"As Irma told you, I was killed a while back. I don't know who did it. But Trixie, as much as I try to get through to her to drop it, won't let it go. And I'm afraid it is going to get her in big trouble. I would like to ask you both to convince Trixie that she should just drop it. That her life is in danger, and I wouldn't want anything to happen to her. In exchange, I will help Irma with her problems."

"Well, Ted ..." I started to tell him that we had better things to do with our time, but there was something about the way Ted looked at me that made my voice falter. He had beautiful eyes. "Look, Ted, we would like to help. But we don't know anything about what happened to you. Or why you were killed."

"It's a long story. I'll tell you at the right time. Just know that I didn't do anything wrong."

I hesitated, but it had to be said, "Well—I'd need to know—I mean—after all, you are in purgatory." I looked at Irma, who had taken up a position next to Ted. I noticed they were the same height.

Irma put her hand on Ted's arm. "Ted's only in purgatory as a way station, like a waiting room. He's free to go through those pearly gates any time he wants."

Up to that point, Lili hadn't said anything. Now she stepped forward. "So Ted, if you don't need to be there, what are you doing in purgatory.?"

"That's easy to explain. I love my wife. Loved her more than anything when I was alive. And love her more now. I'm just keeping an eye on her, and I hope many years from now, we'll be able to walk hand in hand into heaven together. But first, I want her to have a long and happy life. That's why I need your help. Please think about it."

With that, the two ghosts disappeared in a ray of sunshine that peeked through the branches of the tree.

Chapter 7

As I carefully pulled Thor back onto the highway, I looked at Lili. We both looked at the backseat, which remained empty. We were finally alone.

I looked at Groot, whose head was bobbling merrily. "Oh, stop it, Groot. Don't be so cheerful. Irma's got me into another mess."

Lili clicked on the radio. For the remainder of the ride, we listened to country music. It reminded me of Nashville. I wondered how Cecelia was doing. It was too early for morning sickness. I would have to text her to load up on crackers.

A half hour later, I pulled into the parking lot of the casino. The first thing that popped into my head was that it wasn't Las Vegas. Not flashy and over the top like the Strip. Hardly any neon lights.

As we walked toward the casino, I couldn't tell if Lili was excited or not.

"Mabel, let's go in for a quick hand of blackjack. Get it out of my system. Then we'll have lunch and check out the town. I liked those lumberjack shirts Josh got. I'd like to find some matching shirts for Bob and me."

Lili is not a gambler, but I knew she loves to play poker because she is really good at it. I wasn't sure about blackjack. I didn't know much about it. I followed her into the casino. It was brighter than all outdoors and noisy. And all the ding-dong and cling-clang of the slot machines made it exciting. Especially when bells and whistles go off when someone wins a big pot.

Gambling doesn't hold any attraction for me. I don't like to lose hard-earned money.

We passed by a hundred or so slot machines on our way to where the real gambling was going on. Some were the modern kind with video displays, but I noticed some older ones. Classics. I recognized one of them. The kind with cherries. That was always my favorite. I wasn't sure if they took pennies anymore. It had been a long time since I had played the slots.

It only took Lili a minute to figure out the layout, but she knew exactly where she wanted to go—the blackjack tables at the back. I followed her.

There were only three. She watched the dealers for a few minutes and then sat at the last table. I took up a position behind her. Just like you always see in James Bond films. The gorgeous gal standing behind him. Of course, I'd be more of a good luck charm. But Lili had other ideas. She turned to me.

"Mabel, why don't you go play the slots?"

I guess standing behind her was messing with her mojo. So, without further ado, I did. That's when Irma and Ted appeared.

I walked right through Irma. Which always gives me the creeps. It's something I'll never get used to.

"Irma, could you at least give me a warning?"

Irma nodded her head in the direction of the black-jack table. I watched as Ted zipped over and stood behind a man who appeared more intent on something other than playing a round of blackjack. I could see Lili had struck up a conversation with a man sitting next to her.

""Irma, what's Ted doing? He better not try to give Lili some inside information. She won't like that. In fact, she'll be insulted."

"Of course not," Irma said. "Ted is an honorable soul. Probably what got him killed?"

Before we knew it, Ted was back and standing next to us.

"Mabel, do you know who Lili is playing with at the blackjack table?"

"You mean the guy she's sitting next to? No. She likes to chitchat with the other players."

"No, not him. The guy who looks like Vito Corleone."

I looked over and realized he meant the man who wasn't paying attention to the game.

"You mean the one who looks like the godfather?"

Ted zipped back over to the table and again stood behind the guy looking intently at the man sitting next to Lili. He pointed at the guy's head and then zipped back.

I looked at the blackjack table and started to say something. I had to be careful that I wasn't spotted talking to these two spirits. So, I moved over behind a large fern. I felt like wagging my finger at the two spirits who joined me at my station behind the fern, but if anyone saw me, they would think I was nuts.

"He doesn't look like Marlon Brando to me," I said. "Maybe more like Tony Soprano, though."

"Mabel, go back over there and stand where you can hear the conversation," Ted said.

"Lili told me to get lost."

"Do it anyway, Mabel. You can explain it to Lili later. Right now, it's important."

I looked at Ted.

"What are you psychic also?"

"Ted has abilities," Irma said.

"What abilities?" I asked the two and eyed the waitress bringing drinks to Lili's table. Too early for a Cosmo, I decided.

Ted gave me a serious look. "I can see things, like your friend Mary Catherine Mahoney."

"Oh, my lord," I said a little too loud. Mary Catherine Mahoney, or MC, is my CPA back in Florida. She can see things from afar, and certain alphabet agencies are always very interested in that ability of hers.

"So, you can see things from afar. What do they call that? Remote control or something or other?"

"Remote viewing," Ted said. "Yes, I can see impressions about a distant or unseen target. I sense it with my mind. Had that ability when I was alive. Came in handy."

"Did the government get you to work for them, too? Like they do MC?"

Ted gave me the stare, which I knew very well since I've seen it planted on Bob's face whenever he switches to Special Forces mode.

"I graduated with an accounting degree and passed the CPA exam. All four parts first sitting. I went to work for the IRS as a special agent. That's where I met your friend Mary Catherine."

"Holy Moly."

Once again, a little too loud because a server turned to look at me. I waved her off.

"Don't tell me you also know an FBI Agent by the name of Bill Grove?"

"I do," Ted said. "Comes with the territory of being a private investigator."

"Good grief."

Just thinking about Agent Bill gave me a headache. He was a thorn in our side when Lili and I helped Irma solve murders in Savannah and the Badlands.

I watched as Ted zipped over to the table and stood behind the godfather. Irma followed him. I had no choice but to plant myself behind Lili.

She turned and eyed me with a quizzical look on her face. I think she suspected something was up, or I wouldn't have come back so soon.

"I ran out of money," I said loud enough so the other players could hear me.

"Mabel, just be quiet," she whispered.

The man sitting next to her turned his head and gave me a friendly smile. He held out his hand. "The name's Harold."

"Nice to meet you, Harold."

I looked at the man sitting end of the table. He looked downright scary. I just smiled and gave him the little old lady from Pasadena look. He glared at me with an are-you-feeling-lucky-today look.

A few minutes later, after Lili won a few more rounds, I snuck another peek at the godfather. For some reason, I thought he looked familiar. I shivered.

I grabbed that drink, after all. Little did I know I was going to need it.

Because I was at the wrong place at the wrong time.

Chapter 8

Lili continued playing blackjack. And she was winning —big time. She was drawing a crowd, but that didn't bother her. She told me she was able to close everything off around her when she played cards. Like she drew a curtain around the card table. But she could still carry on a conversation. She shared this with me and how to play blackjack during our ride to the casino.

"Blackjack is the most popular and most played casino game in the entire world. It's also known as twenty-one. In most casinos, they use six to eight decks of cards. As you know, Mabel, the goal is to get as close to twenty-one without going over."

"How much do you wager? Lili, you know I don't like losing money."

"Then, Mabel, I don't think you should play. Because you must be quick. Decide when to stand. That means not taking another card. Or when to hit. Only do that when the dealer has a card between seven and an ace. And always, always split aces and eights. Or double eleven or hit an ace. You win if the value of the cards in your hand is higher than the dealers or equal to twenty-one. If the value of your hand is lower than the dealers or crosses twenty-one, you'll lose your wager to the dealer."

"You lost me back at 'be quick'—I'll stick to the slots."

My brain was basically mush with stuff like learning how to play cards or even figuring the amount of a tip I should add to a bill at a restaurant. I like it when the bill comes with your choices.

I had watched Lili play poker. I knew chatting was all part of the strategy of the game. Distract your opponent. She told me it was very psychological.

I didn't know if it also worked in blackjack, where I think players try to count cards. Lili and Harold were chitchatting away, but I noticed they never took their eyes off the cards.

But poor Harold was at the wrong place wrong time. The godfather across the table would see to that shortly.

Unfortunately for Lili, she was also at the wrong place wrong time.

Chapter 9

"What do you mean Lili was arrested for murder? Am I in a parallel universe?"

Standing in front of me was Jolene, Lili's twin. In a richly embroidered purple African kaftan, she looked as imposing as she sounded. They were so different they could have been born in alternate universes.

A split second ago, her big black SUV had pulled up and parked in front of our campers. I was still wearing my Donald Duck PJs and robe when I peeked out the window. I didn't have time to change, so I unlocked the door and poured myself a cup of coffee. Too early to add a little Kahlua. I didn't have long to wait. Her two men, who not too long ago played for the NFL, opened the door of the SUV and helped her out. Ten seconds later, she burst through my door.

I had decided to stay cool. She had enough nervous energy for both of us. "Hello Jolene, can I get you a cup of coffee? Some of Lili's cinnamon coffee cake?"

I felt a little underdressed in my PJs, so I reached over and put on my matching Minnie Mouse robe.

Toto, who had been sleeping in my lazy girl chair, woke up. When he stood up on his two hind feet, he scared the bejeezus out of Jolene. She had seen my poor prairie dog back in the Badlands, but his sharp, high bark seemed to unnerve her.

Not everyone takes to prairie dogs.

"Ugh! What's that rat doing here? I thought you would have dumped him by now. You certainly drove through enough prairie land on your way here."

"I couldn't dump him. And he's not a rat. He's related to squirrels. In any case, I don't know where his family is. He's now my emotional support prairie dog. His name is Toto."

Toto was circling her. I could see they were both at a standoff, and neither was going to stand down.

"Toto, say hello to your Aunt Jolene," I said as I leaned down and picked Toto up and placed him in my arms. He stopped snippy barking and relaxed for a second, and then jumped out of my arms and stood right next to my Donald Duck slippers. An impasse.

Jolene kept a wary eye on him and then looked at me. "I'll take some of that coffee, black, trying to cut back—and a small piece of Lili's coffee cake."

Progress, I thought as I poured Jolene a cup of coffee and cut a small piece of coffee cake, and brought it over to Jolene. I placed it down on my coffee table, and she plunked down on my sofa and took a sip of coffee.

"Didn't have time for breakfast. We drove here non-stop." She took a bite of the coffee cake. "Lili knows how to bake. I'll give her that."

Jolene wiped the crumbs from her lips with a nap-
kin and then stood up.

"Well, grasshopper, what's the story?"

About that time, things went from bad to worse.
Irma showed up! Dressed from top to bottom in black
leather and she was carrying her whip. She had several
in different sizes. This was her biggest one. She got
close to Jolene and cracked it next to her. I almost
jumped off my chair.

"Is that ghost lady here?"

"Can you see her?"

"I can see you and Mabel. You can't hide anything,
so never play poker."

Irma continued to circle around Jolene, and now
Toto joined her.

"Tell her what's going on," Irma said as she pointed
the whip in my direction.

I got up and poured myself another cup of coffee,
sat down and closed my eyes, made the sign of the
cross even though I was Jewish, and told Jolene why
Lili was arrested.

"Lili's been arrested for murdering this guy named
Harold, who she was sitting right next to her at the
blackjack table. As I told you when I called, she's in
the local jail. Bob is already on top of things. The first
thing he did was talk with the sheriff, who, lucky for
us, turned out to be a Marine. He was in Desert Storm.
Anyway, he's going out of his way to make sure Lili is
as comfortable as one can be stuck in a jail cell."

Jolene placed her hands on her well-endowed hips

and started tapping her feet. Irma had changed into her nun's habit, but she still had that whip.

I walked over and poured a small shot of Kahlua into my coffee. It's five o'clock somewhere. I could hear Jolene—tap-tap and then a double tap-tap. Like morse code. I sat back down. Mother superior was braced to crack that whip or maybe strangle someone with her thick rosary that had beads the size of ping-pong balls.

"Mabel, how did my sister get mixed up in this mess? We all know Lili doesn't even like to squash bugs. Arrested for murder? That's crazy?"

"Well, Jolene, we don't know the full story yet. Only that Lili's gun was found next to Harold's body. He was in witness protection but was getting careless. Took chances. Became lackadaisical about security, and he loved gambling, or at least, he loved being among people. He was lonely. Lost his wife several years ago."

"We went to the casino in Central City. We dropped in the casino for a quick look around. Lili said she would check out the blackjack game, and then we were going to go to lunch and do some shopping."

"Hmm, so she took my suggestion to go to a casino? She plays a little blackjack and then gets arrested for murder," Jolene rubbed her forehead and sighed. "Dang. It's my fault."

I now saw something I had not seen before. Genuine emotion and concern for her twin. Usually, they're fighting like cats and dogs because Jolene is sure that Lili stole Carl away from her. The truth was,

Lili did. But I was sworn to secrecy, and that secret would go with me to my grave unless Jolene used some waterboarding techniques on me.

"It's not your fault, Jolene. We were just in the wrong place at the wrong time."

Jolene closed her eyes for a moment. I stayed silent as it looked to me like she was praying.

Irma rolled her eyes, and the whip disappeared, but in its place was a ruler. A big one, and it was pointed at me—right under my nose.

"Mabel, tell Jolene to get on the ball. Help us get to the bottom of this. Find out who murdered this guy, Harold, and save Lili."

Jolene opened her eyes. "I agree with the ghost lady."

"Wait, a minute. You can hear Irma?"

"Yeah, don't know why. This isn't the miracle I was praying for. But it will do. When we were kids, Lili and I could both see our cat Kiki who died. And our favorite auntie. After a while, we lost the knack. What kid wants to see dead people? But now it's back, and yeah, I see you, Irma. What's up with that nun's habit?"

"I've been praying, too," Irma said to Jolene and pointed the ruler in her direction.

"I can see you've got a sense of humor. Okay, ghost lady, you and I and Mabel are a team. We need to find out who killed this guy, how they got their hands on Lili's gun, and let's get this done before Bob finds out I'm here. I'll be staying at that hotel in Estes Park. It's called the Stanley Hotel. And they say it's haunted."

"You don't want to stay there," Irma said, pointing that darn ruler closer at Jolene.

"Why not? You afraid of ghosts?" Jolene said with a little too much snark in her voice.

Chapter 10

Before Jolene could leave, there was a knock on my camper door, and Bob walked in. He stopped in mid-stride and looked at Jolene.

"Jolene."

"Bob."

Bob looked tired. He hadn't gotten much sleep since Lili was taken away, and the stress was starting to show. Nevertheless, Bob pulled himself together as you would expect from someone with his experience. He's been in tough situations before. He could be as cool and focused as Harry Bosch. But I knew that this was something special. It was against every grain of his long law enforcement career to stand in the same room with Jolene, who ran an operation on the other side of the line. I had once asked Lili what Jolene did— it was obviously less than kosher. But Lili doesn't blab.

"Mabel, it's better you don't know. Her services are expensive and useful to some people. But she is on a razor-thin edge, and if things ever go really wrong, I don't know what would happen to her. Bob did tell me that he would give her a head start if it ever came down to it."

Jolene looked like she was doing everything she could to not pull out a gun if Bob made a move. I knew she was packing. It was somewhere underneath the colorful embroidered African kaftan she was wearing. She had a scarf wrapped around her head that matched her purple kaftan. Maybe she had the gun hidden in her scarf?

If it wasn't for the bond between them—both of them loved Lili more than anything in the world—they would not be in the same room together. Actually, no one in their right mind would stand in Bob's Airstream with the two of them, but here we were.

"We're about to have company," Bob said to us.

There was a knock on the door, and Bob opened it. The man who walked in was wearing a black windbreaker emblazoned with US Marshal in big white letters on the back.

As if the place wasn't crowded enough, Irma and Ted decided to put in an appearance.

I peeked out the window. Several black SUVs with government licenses had joined Jolene's SUVs. It was not surprising that all the action had attracted a crowd. Worst of all, Peggy was engaging with them since the government types, and Jolene's linebackers stood in stoic silence. I hated to think about what she was telling them.

Things were about to go from bad to worse when my phone dinged, and I looked down to see a text from Bianca: ON MY WAY! She always uses exclamation

gumshoe. So, he did a u-turn and followed the van. What happened next surprised him. The van went only a few miles before turning onto a side road. Harold knew the area. There was no good reason for anyone to drive into the woods in the dark. So, after pulling into a dirt road, Harold hiked a little ways through the woods. The van door was open, and the customer was digging a grave. Harold didn't dare move when the guy reached into the van, pulled out the tarp, and dumped it into the hole."

"Wow," said Bianca. "He must have been frightened."

Marshal Cohen looked at her, "Yes, m ... miss. He was that. But he did snap some shots as the guy filled in the grave and covered it with broken branches. As soon as it was safe, Harold called the police. They found the body and arrested the guy just as he was leaving the seedy motel."

Jolene interrupted. "So that's how Harold became the key witness in a mob murder trial?"

"Yes, ma'am. The body turned out to be a woman who was a blackjack dealer. She was at the wrong place wrong time. Surveillance cameras show her leaving the casino. She stopped to light a cigarette. Two men came around a corner. They were arguing. Obviously, a conversation that should not have been overheard. When they saw her, they stopped. She quickly walks past them, but that's the last time she was seen. We surmised that they decided to take care of her. The guy Harold identified was the one who killed her and was sent to prison—where he was knocked off. I guess what comes around goes around. And the mob is unforgiving."

"So, what does this have to do with Lili?" Bob asked.

"We believe that the brother of the man Harold identified in court is the one who was at the blackjack table with Lili. That's the guy who killed Harold. And has framed Lili. Like I said, mob guys have long memories."

I stood up. My hands were shaking. "So it looks like Lili and I were in the wrong place at the wrong time."

I could hear Jolene suck in her breath.

The Marshal nodded his head and turned to Bob. "I'm afraid so. That's why we can't help your wife right now. We need you all to be patient. Once the brother is found, he will be arrested. Then your wife will be released. You just need for all of you to be patient."

"My patience is running thin. Every minute Lili spends in jail is ripping me apart. And I'm sorry, Marshal Cohen, but there's more to this than what you're telling us. What is it? My guess it's the FBI — have something they want from him?"

Bianca spoke up now. "Please tell us. My Aunt Lili, who I love dearly, is a good and decent woman. This should not be happening to her. She never hurt anyone. She's one of the kindest souls I've ever met."

Marshal Cohen was looking at Bianca. She had tears flowing like gushers from those beautiful blue eyes of hers. She was trembling. I almost thought he was going to walk over and wrap her in his arms. He shook his head. Took a deep breath and, against his better judgment, revealed some more information to us.

"I shouldn't be telling you this, but I don't like this whole setup—leaving someone sitting in jail for a crime they didn't commit rubs me the wrong way. I suspect, but don't know for sure, that the FBI has been talking to him. I can't tell you his name, but I suspect he is high up on the fruit tree. Probably has a lot of information that would be extremely valuable to the FBI. In return, they more than likely will offer him a deal. They'll get what they can out of him and then put him in WitSec. Once they get him to agree and they have the information, Lili will be released. That makes him a time bomb for the mob. He knows he's running out of time. Shooting Harold was a big mistake. He should have never done that. Called so much attention to himself and the mob. Over the years, Harold and I became friends. He did the right thing all those years ago. But I warned him he needed to be careful. It's sad, but once he lost his wife, he wouldn't listen. He was tired and wanted his life back. Or maybe he knew what he was doing and just wanted it over with—just wanted to join her."

Marshal Cohen got up and handed Bianca a Kleenex from a nearby box.

"Thank you," she said.

"Yes, ma'am. Oh sorry. My bad."

"It's okay," Bianca said and smiled at him.

He looked like he was going to melt into the floor.

I looked at Bob and Jolene, who exchanged a look between them. From that look, I knew a truce had been declared, and a pact was forged between them to do whatever they had to do to free Lili.

"Sorry, Marshal, I'm not the patient type," Bob repeated. He went over and unlocked the camper door and held it open. "But thank you, son, for sharing that information."

Marshal Cohen looked around the room and nodded his head. His eyes lingered on Bianca for a few moments.

He reached his hand out to Bob. "Copy that, sir."

Bob stood at the door of the camper and watched as the government SUVs pulled out of the campground.

Chapter 11

"They can't do this," Jolene said. She was back to pacing back and forth the length of my Airstream. She was raising her fists and punching a virtual boxing bag.

"They can if they have bigger fish to fry," Bob said.

"Bob, what are we going to do?"

Bob didn't respond. He seemed lost in thought at the idea that Lili might be sitting in jail for a while until the FBI could reel in the mobster who shot Harold.

I walked over to my compact little kitchen area. "Look, I'm going to put on a fresh pot of coffee, and then we'll all put on our thinking caps. Bob, sit down, and I'll give you one of Lili's peanut butter cookies. Lucky she always makes sure my cookie jar is filled."

He gave me a thin smile and sat down. "It's simple and not so simple. What we need is evidence that proves this mobster got his hands on Lili's gun and used it to shoot Harold."

"But in the meantime, what about Aunt Lili? She's sitting in jail," Bianca said.

"Bob, why don't you call our old friend in the FBI—Agent Bill; Let's see what he can do without revealing what Marshal Cohen told us about the FBI's interest in this matter."

"Good idea, Mabel. I'll do it right now." Bob got up and stepped outside.

"I'm heading back to the hotel," Jolene said when she stopped her pacing. "It was great to meet you, Bianca. I've heard a lot about you. We'll have to get to know each other a little better while you are visiting Mabel."

"I'd like that," Bianca said.

With that, Jolene left along with her NFL body-guards. The campground was no longer full of black SUVs.

Bob came back in, and I handed him a cup of coffee, which he obviously needed. He was running on empty. "I spoke with Bill—he sends you his regards, Mabel—and no surprise, he's familiar with everything going on. He said as soon as he got off the phone, he'd arrange to have Lili transferred and put under FBI protection. She'll be safer, and he apologized profusely for the unfortunate predicament of Lili being in the crosshairs of this FBI matter."

"Safer? What does that mean?" Bianca asked. She was also sipping a cup of coffee. I figured she must be tired.

"Agent Bill is concerned," Bob said. I could tell by his voice that he was as shaken by the idea of Lili being in danger as Bianca and I were. "He says the mob might come back and tie up loose ends."

"Oh no, Bob. Does that mean Lili and this other mob boss are in the crosshairs?"

Bob nodded his head, and I clearly saw the fear in his eyes. He gulped down the rest of his coffee and accepted one of Lili's cookies. He looked at it for a moment, and I thought he was going to burst into tears. Instead, he ate it in two bites, and I realized he probably hadn't eaten all day.

"Bob, we must find some way to prove Lili did not shoot Harold. It will take her out of the mob's bulls' eye and put the heat where it belongs. That mobster who shot Harold."

Irma and Ted had been quiet during this exchange. She had changed into her meter maid outfit. "Mabel, stay strong. Lili needs you. Ted and I are going to investigate it. Right, Ted?"

Ted smiled at me and nodded his head. Somehow, I found it very reassuring.

"Roger that," I said.

Bianca turned to look at me. "Did you say something, Mom?"

"Me?" I squeaked. "No, I was just saying you must be tired. And so are you, Bob. It won't help Lili if you collapse. Go and get some sleep. We'll start fresh in the morning."

* * *

Before Bob left to go to his own Airstream, he lifted Bianca's luggage into my camper,

Toto absolutely adored her from the get-go, and Bianca adored him.

I poured myself a cup of coffee. I was also running out of steam and hoped that Bob would be able to fall asleep. "So, are you planning on moving in?"

"No, Mom. I brought clothes and my walking poles. I plan for us to do some walking, and I brought you a pair of walking poles."

With that, she walked over and snapped open one piece of luggage, and out came two sets of walking poles. "Mom, you are in the Rocky Mountains. It's a great place to hike."

"Bianca, it'll be fun to join you. I've been getting behind on my walking. Although I have done a lot of walking on this adventure of mine with Betsy and Thor."

"Who?"

"Betsy is my camper, and Thor is my F-150," I said.

"Oh, that's cute. But Betsy? How did you come up with that name?"

Irma suddenly showed up. She tells me that she doesn't eavesdrop on me, but sometimes I wonder how she knew when to show up. Do a ghost's ears ring when someone talks about them?

"Well, the camper comes with a sad story. A long time ago, a previous owner, also named Walt and in law enforcement like the Marshal we met today, had a hit out on him. His mother showed up and took the bullet for him and saved his life."

"Really? That is a sad story," Bianca said. "She was Betsy?"

"No. Her name is Irma, and she gave him up at birth and he was raised by her sister, whose name was Betsy."

"Why did she give him up?"

"Well, she was a madam of a bordello in Las Vegas. Not a good place to raise a child."

"She sounds like quite a strong woman."

"Very strong. But I thought you had strong opinions about women's rights and women working as hookers."

"Oh, I do, but those women can't be blamed for finding themselves in that life. It'll be cool to meet someone like Irma."

"Well, Bianca, you just might. You just might."

"Is that so? Does she live around here?"

"Something like that," I said. "Something like that."

I looked over at Irma, who was beaming.

"Tell her," Irma said, and then she vanished to give Bianca and me time to visit. Over some wine, I told her all about Irma. Might as well. Hard to hide a ghost who lives in your camper. To my surprise, Bianca took it very well.

Chapter 12

Bianca still had not told me the reason for her visit, and since I've known her since the minute she was born, I knew it wasn't only to visit dear old Mom. I wasn't going to come right out and ask, but I was dropping hints.

But we were both tired, and it would have to wait until morning.

The next morning, we were up early and were enjoying the early morning breeze. I enjoyed the quiet as we sipped our coffee and watched the um rise. It was going to be a beautiful day.

"If Lili were here, we would be treated to her blueberry muffins." I went inside to warm up some cinnamon coffee cake.

Earlier, we had heard Bob go out for a ride on his Harley. The distinct sound of a Harley-Davidson is like nothing else in the world.

Peggy and Josh were not up yet. Late sleepers.

I looked over at my beautiful daughter. "So, Bianca, is Henry watching the cupcake factory?"

"Yes, he and Barry are covering for me while I visit with you. Barry is between stunt gigs right now, and so he has a week or so to help out."

"I really like Barry," I said. "They make a nice couple."

"They do," Bianca agreed as she nibbled on the coffee cake. "Mom…"

Here it comes. She was about to tell me the real reason she was visiting, and I knew it wasn't to go hiking or mountain climbing. There was a reason for her visit. I could sense it.

"I'm thinking of having a baby."

I swallowed my coffee, and as the saying goes, it went down the wrong pipe, and I started coughing. Bianca was slapping me on my back as the coffee came out of my nose. She ran into the camper and brought me a bottle of water and a tissue. I took a minute to drink some water until I could talk again.

"Mom, are you okay now? I didn't intend for you to choke on your coffee!" she said with a sheepish grin. "Sorry to spring it on you, but I'm close to turning thirty, and I think it's time."

I didn't know what to say. Reminded me of when I had the birds and the bees discussion with my kids. I took care of our girls, and Jack covered our boys. She was looking at me now for a response, and that's when Irma showed up. She was holding a pink plastic flamingo and was wearing a white lab coat. Bianca looked in the direction of where I was staring at Irma. She didn't say anything and then looked back at me.

"Bianca, having a child as a single mother is

something I think you should consider very, very seriously. You know I'm old-fashioned. Marriage and then children."

"I haven't met someone I want to spend the rest of my life with, and I don't know if I ever will. I'm busy with my business. I don't have time to date."

"Well, a baby is a 24/7 deal. How are you going to find time for a baby? The first year, they keep you up at night."

"When the baby is born, I'm taking the first six months off. Henry can run the business, and I'll work part-time."

"Have you discussed that with Henry?"

"I wanted to talk to you first. That's why I'm here."

Like whatever I thought would make a difference. "Bianca, I love you, and I will stand by you no matter what your decision is, but I'd suggest you take some time to consider going through this life-changing event alone. Give it some time. Maybe even start dating again. Who knows, you might meet the father of your future children?"

I wanted to say I saw the way you and the US Marshal looked at each other but held back.

"I was hoping to have this discussion with you and Aunt Lili."

Right about then, we heard the distinct roar of Bob's Harley and watched as he parked his bike and came over to join us. He looked at our faces. "Good morning, Mabel. Bianca. I didn't mean to interrupt something. I can come back later…"

"No, Bob, stay. I'll get you a cup of coffee." As I

went inside, Bob pulled up a chair next to Bianca. I noticed that she put her hand on his."

When I came back, I handed Bob a mug of steaming coffee and a piece of the coffee cake. "Bob, when can we go see Lili?"

"They're moving her from the jail now. As soon as she's settled, we'll go see her. She'll be happy to hear the great news." He looked at Bianca and smiled.

"Great news?" I looked from Bob to Bianca. I noticed that she was blushing.

"Mom. I was just telling Bob that I'm pregnant."

Chapter 13

By the look on my face—my jaw must have dropped—
Bianca gave me a little smile. Bob decided it was time to
leave us alone and excused himself to go in and shower.
He announced that he would drive us a little later.

I turned to Bianca. She shrugged her shoulders.
"Something about Bob makes a person want to confess.
He must have been great in an interrogation room. But
Mom, I had planned to break the news slowly. I guess
you're a bit shocked?"

"To put it mildly," I said and reached for her hand.
"But I'm happy for you. And for me. You'll make a
wonderful mother. So, when can we expect this bundle
of joy? And who is the father?"

Irma now to the opportunity to show up. And she
was holding two plastic flamingos.

"What?" I said to Irma, not thinking.

"Breathe in—Breathe out," she said, holding the two
pink flamingos in her arms like babies.

Bianca was looking at me and then toward where I
was looking.

"Are you okay, Mom?"

"Yeah. I'm just talking to myself. None of my business how you got pregnant. I think I know how it happens after five kids."

In her typical matter-of-fact fashion, Bianca told me who the father was, "Mom, a good friend of Henry's, agreed to be the sperm donor."

"One of Henry's friends is the father?"

My mind was still reeling, and I couldn't bring myself to say *sperm donor* because the only way I know to bring children into this world has been around since the dawn of time.

"How does that work? Never mind. TMI."

"He's an actor on Broadway. And no, Mom, by the look in your eyes, I did not become pregnant the old fashion way, if that's what you are thinking. Anyway, he's gay."

With that, Bianca pulled out a picture from her shorts pocket and showed it to me. "This is the father. His name is Roger."

She handed me the picture, and I was looking at one drop-dead gorgeous, handsome man. He had the looks for the stage or the movies or Netflix. He was tall and had broad shoulders. Dark hair, dark eyes, and a muscular build. He was smiling in the picture. Beautiful teeth.

"Well, with your looks and the father's, the baby is going to be absolutely gorgeous."

"I can't wait for you to meet your next grandchild."

"Me too," Irma said, still holding those pink flamingos.

I looked at Irma and gave her a wink. I'm glad it

made Irma happy. I hoped that we would be able to take Irma to see her son and grandchildren.

With that, I reached over and hugged my most independent millennial daughter, and so did Irma.

"I needed that, Mom," and then she had a sudden inexplicable shiver. I could see goose bumps on her arms.

"Someone walking on my grave?"

Something my Aunt Sadie used to say years ago when I was a child. She's the one who explained my ability to see dead people was a gift. I was surprised that Bianca remembered.

"No. Just your hormones. So, you haven't told your father?"

"No, I wanted to tell you first, and Aunt Lili."

We hugged again, and Irma gave us a thumbs up with a grin.

"You don't look pregnant, and if I were you, I'd stop wearing those Choo Choo heels. You don't want to fall."

"It's Jimmy Choo, Mabel," Irma corrected me.

How would I know? I buy my shoes at Walmart anymore.

"Bianca, let's go for a walk. I want to try out that walking stick."

* * *

When we returned from our walk, Bob was ready to take us. Of course, we both became overly protective of pregnant Bianca. I put a small pillow behind her back. She just rolled her eyes at our attentiveness. But I had a feeling she enjoyed it.

No sooner than we got her situated, Irma appeared, sitting right next to her, and was dressed in the nurse's uniform from the 1960s. Way before scrubs—starched white dress, white nylons, and white shoes, and the universally recognized symbol of nursing from that era was sitting on her head—a white cap. Irma gave me the hand wave that said, "move along—nothing to see here."

So far, it looked as if Bianca had not inherited the—I see dead people genes—like her sister Cecilia, who we discovered in Nashville could see Irma. I hoped it stayed that way.

Bob dropped us off in front of the hotel, parked his truck, and met us in the lobby. The three of us went up the elevator. I noticed we went to the top floor. We followed Bob down the hallway to what obviously was Lili's room because there were FBI types guarding the door, and sitting close by were Jolene's men. They all had that look and the buzz haircut. "High and tight," is what Bob called it. Bob nodded at the two guards, and they stepped aside to let Bob open the door wide.

We saw Lili sitting at a table, blowing on her fingers. A manicurist was packing up her supplies.

Bianca went over to Lili and, careful not to smudge her nails, gave Lili a big hug.

"Oh, Bianca. You look gorgeous. Love the hair!" Lili said as she waved her hands in the air. "Your pregnant!"

"Yes," Bianca said gleefully, followed by more hugs between the two.

"Wait a minute, Lili. Did Bob already tell you? How did you know she was pregnant?"

"Oh, Mabel, just look at her complexion and eyes," Lili said and gave Bob and me a hug.

"Wow," Bianca said and walked over to the floor-to-ceiling windows with an out-of-this-world view of the Rocky Mountains.

"Sit. Sit. Can I get you anything? I can call room service."

We took a minute to sit, and then Bob said, "Mabel, this suite was arranged by our friend from the FBI."

"Really. Agent Bill arranged for a penthouse suite. He must have been in a good mood." I looked around the beautiful room. It had a small kitchen and a bar. There was a bank of two couches and some comfortable chairs. The view of the Rocky Mountains from the top-to-bottom windows was truly spectacular. I got up and peeked into the bedroom and luxurious bathroom. Well, at least Lili would be comfortable.

Agent Bill had been a thorn in my side, but now I had to re-think that. This certain bumped him up in my estimation. So he had obviously gotten over Lili and me stepping on his toes a few times. Anyway, in the end, we did make him look good by solving a few murders along the way.

"Bill is a good guy. He's concerned for Lili's safety. He convinced the higher-ups that if they wanted cooperation, they would have to do right by her. And Harold"

"I only spoke with Harold for a bit, but he seemed like a nice guy," Lili said with sadness. "They think I'm safer in custody here. I heard the US Marshal came by and talked with all of you."

Chapter 14

Bianca and I were back at the camper, and she decided to take a nap. I went outside and sat underneath my awning in the shade so I wouldn't disturb her nap. I didn't see Bob's Harley. That told me he was out riding.

Peggy and Josh were absent. They usually stayed inside their ice-cold camper during the afternoons. It was getting close to happy hour time, but with Lili's absence, it didn't seem very happy. Lili always made the best hors d'oeuvres, so there was that. Peggy offered to make pigs in a blanket. But there were just so many pigs in a blanket one could eat. I made my cocktail meatballs. My go-to recipe over the years, but lately, we'd stopped meeting for happy hour. Lili's absence was woefully missed, and not just because she was a great cook. Maybe Bianca will do some baking while she visits. A dozen of her famous cupcakes would be fun and cheer us up. We could make them together like we did when she was a little girl with lots of sprinkles.

I sat there and closed my eyes and, of course, when I opened them—there was Irma—the ghost in my camper. She was wearing her showgirl outfit—minus the headdress and feathers—black rhinestone fishnet tights and spiked black heels, which made her half a foot taller.

"Traditionally, Las Vegas showgirls were classically trained dancers with skills in ballet and jazz dance," Irma had informed me soon after we met. "Most of the girls had an impressive dance pedigree, starting with classical ballet."

"And you?" I remember asking. "Were you classically trained?"

"Nope, not classical, but I could dance. What gave me an edge was I was insanely tall–6-2" and most of my height was in my very long legs," she said and then showed me some high kicks with those long legs. "Couldn't be short like you, Mabel. I was also physically strong. Had to be to wear sky-high heels, a feathered headdress that could weigh up to 30 pounds, and bejeweled costumes and prance around a stage for at least 90 minutes. Not everyone was up to that. As a new dancer, I went through three to four weeks of intense training to make sure I could physically carry the load, not to mention memorizing thousands of dance combinations. Turns out I could prance around for hours, and the dance steps came naturally to me. We had six to eight costume changes per show, by the way."

I was soon to learn that Irma loved to change outfits and was a quick-change artist.

"So, Irma, I may have to make a trip back home and peek into my safe deposit box. See if that mob guy who shot Harold was a patient of Jack's."

"We got our work cut out for us," Irma said, and then the tall showgirl started strutting back and forth in front of me.

I got up and peeked in my camper to make sure Bianca was still napping. Although I had told Bianca about Irma, I left out some parts. These murder mysteries that Lili and I had tripped over on the trip were directly related to helping Irma get out of purgatory. I was going to wait for the next glass of wine before I told her the rest of the story.

"We need to figure out how that mobster got his hands on Lili's gun. The one he used to shoot Harold and then left next to poor Harold's dead body. It needs to be done before they ship Lili and Bob off to witness protection."

As Irma did a pivot in front of me, she leaned over and smothered me with her feathers. I sneezed.

"He picked up from the conversation at the blackjack table that Lili's gun was a Ruger P95 pistol. Broke in the camper, took the gun, shot Harold," said the tall showgirl prancing back and forth in front of me. "And framed Lili."

"Being a godfather, he would not have been the one to break into the camper and shoot Harold. He would have had one of his men do the job."

"I'm sure the sheriff who arrested Lili would have asked if anyone saw anything?" Irma said.

"It's a big campground. People coming and going. I could talk to Al, the manager of the campground. I've seen him on his golf cart making his rounds."

Right then, we both looked at each other.

"Maybe Al needs to be looked at a little closer. Ask Bob to check out his background."

"Roger that."

"By the way, while you are out and about, can you drop in and check on Ted's wife, Trixie? Ted is concerned that she is way over her head trying to find out who shot Ted."

"Sure. What's one more murder to solve? Does Ted have any idea who shot him?"

"I think he knows who shot him. It's not like he can do anything about it now. He's more concerned about his wife, Trixie. She's all alone now, and the grief is overwhelming."

"Where can I find her?"

"Actually, she's a dealer at the same casino, Lili, and you went to the other day."

"She is?"

"After Ted died, she found herself drinking and eating—emotionally. So, she took a course to learn how to be a card dealer. She works at the casino part-time but lives in Estes Park. It keeps her mind sharp, and she gets out and about. Not looking at four walls."

"Okay, I'll drop in and say hello. Where does she live?"

"Don't have a clue. But Ted said if you hop in your truck, he'll guide us."

"Well, I promised Bianca we'd go shopping. Her clothes are snug. Just be incognito."

Bianca stuck her head out the door of the camper.

"Mom, did I hear you talking to someone?"

"No, dear. Talking to myself."

Bianca came out and sat down next to me. "You do that a lot, you know?"

She was looking at me, and then she looked toward Irma, standing nearby. She had added the headdress and more feathers. Lots of feathers. Those poor birds.

"You know, while I was sleeping, I opened my eyes, and I thought I saw your ghost. It was weird."

"How do you know it was my ghost? Lots of ghosts in these here parts."

"Well, you said she was a showgirl, and she had that Vegas showgirl outfit on. Does that happen to you?"

I took a deep breath and decided what the heck. If it was Margaret, there was no way I'd be telling her about Irma.

"Bianca, I do. On my side of the family, we can see dead people."

Bianca once again had those big blue eyes wide open.

"Really?"

"You were too little to meet your great Aunt Sadie, but she explained what was going on when I kept seeing dead relatives and pets. I guess it's a gene that runs in our family."

"Do you think I have that gene?"

"Have you seen any dead people lately?"

"Sometimes, I think I see something out of the corner of my eye at the cupcake factory, like a shadow. It's an ancient building. Who else in our family has that gene?"

"Your sister Cecilia sure does. She saw Irma right off the bat."

Irma had changed into pedal pushers, as she called them, and a white short-sleeved blouse.

"Is she here?"

"Yep."

"Hello, Irma? Nice to meet you."

"Hello, Bianca. The pleasure is all mine."

"Irma says hello. She is stuck in purgatory and has a long sentence. If she does good deeds for the living, Saint Peter gives her extra credit. Solving murders is at the top of the list."

"No kidding. So, you and Aunt Lili have been helping her out?"

"I have little choice. Solving murders brings her one step closer to walking through the gates of heaven and out the door of my camper."

"Cool. While I'm visiting, I'd like to help."

"Well, we sort of have to with Lili being charged for the murder of Harold. Plus, she has a new friend, and his name is Ted. He was a private detective, and he was murdered. Irma asked me to drop in and visit his wife, Trixie. She's apparently bent on solving his murder, and this concerns her friend Ted. If we check in on her and make sure she doesn't wind up with Irma and Ted, he has promised to assist Irma on cases."

"Mom, this is so fascinating. You've come a long way..."

Bianca stopped mid-sentence.

"Since your father left me for Tiffanie?"

My five kids tiptoe around the fact that their father dumped me for someone close to the same age as Bianca. I decided early on not to trash their father in front of them. It would have put them in a position of choosing sides. Didn't need that. I knew where they stood with what their father did.

"Mom, I admire you, not bashing, Dad. He certainly deserves it."

"No need to. Karma is seeing to that."

"Did you ever think of becoming a guardian to the twins?" I asked her.

Tiffanie left Jack with a set of twins. Motherhood impeded a boyfriend closer to her age. My kids told me she had a boyfriend all along. Karma was working overtime on Jack. I believe in karma.

"I did, but Dad said he was keeping the twins. Plus, I think Dad should learn how to change diapers."

We sat there for a minute. Irma had disappeared. Giving Bianca and me time to talk.

Bob came out and started setting up the grill. Peggy and Josh appeared and came over to say hello to Bianca. As soon as I made the introductions, Josh excused himself to go help Bob. Peggy immediately glued herself to Bianca, asking questions about hair, nails, and make-up. Bianca gave me a quizzical look when Peggy got up and walked over to Josh and Bob.

"She and Josh are on this trip to put a little spark back into the marriage."

"Oh," Bianca said. She spent most of the evening happily giving Peggy all kinds of tips—I listened attentively. Doesn't hurt, as my Aunt Sadie used to say.

Chapter 15

We heard someone knocking on our camper door. I looked at Bianca, and she looked at me. We had just said our nighty-night. We were both tired and called it a night about the time Peggy asked Bianca to do her make-up. She had gone shopping today at Walmart and picked up some cosmetics. Bianca promised to take her instead to the mall. Bianca didn't buy cosmetics at the drugstore like I have all my life.

I got up and looked out my window and saw a woman who looked to be about my age pulling out her cell phone. Maybe she had the wrong camper? Geez.

"It's some woman. She might have the wrong camper. Go back to sleep. I'll go outside and see what's going on."

I opened the door and carefully went down the doorsteps. Didn't need to fall. A full moon illuminated the campground. The woman was looking at her cell phone. She looked at me and stuck the cell phone in a purse the size of a small piece of luggage. Probably lost forever.

"Are you Mabel Gold?"

"Whose asking."

"I'm Trixie. Can you help me? I need to find out who murdered my husband, Ted."

"Ahhh. How did you find me?"

"That ghost Irma, who's been hanging around my husband Ted, told me where to find you."

"You know Irma?" I looked around, but Irma was suspiciously absent.

"As well as one could know someone who's dead, you know—a ghost."

Looking at this woman, I was sorry I had one too many glasses of wine. She was about 5 feet even and very tiny. She was wearing jeans with a floral print embroidered on them and a matching jacket with wine-colored boots. Her hair was short and all white, not the white your hair color would go gradually if you let the gray grow out. Something I was considering. Trixie's hair was silver white and styled to frame her pixie face beautifully.

I pointed to the lawn chairs outside of my camper. "Please, why don't you have a seat? My daughter's asleep. She's pregnant."

"Oh, thank you. I'll whisper," she said as she politely lowered her voice and sat down.

Have you ever met someone, and you feel like you've known them for ages? I immediately felt like Trixie and I could be friends.

"How many months is she?"

"I'm not sure. She just told me that she's pregnant. Her biological clock was ticking loudly, and she decided she wasn't waiting any longer for Prince Charming to show. She's my youngest."

"I have a daughter just like her. A real free spirit. Unconventional."

"I know what that is. She doesn't happen to own a cupcake factory?"

"No. A food truck. She and Ted were so close. They..." her voice quivered as she reached into her purse and pulled out some Kleenex. Her green eyes were as puffy as marshmallows. "They were so close."

I put my fingers to my lips and pointed to my camper. "I'm going to sneak in a grab some waters." I didn't add that I needed it because I had the extra glass of wine.

I gave her hand a little squeeze before I handed her a bottle of water.

"Trixie, I'm so sorry. I know it's not the same, but I lost my husband, too—in a pretty bitter divorce. But we had been married over forty years, and it still hurts. So I know the feeling of loss and how overwhelming it can be." This time she gave my hand a squeeze.

I added, "My husband dumped me for a Tiffanie."

"I hate Tiffanies," Trixie said between sniffles. "Was she a bimbo?"

This made us both smile. "Pretty much. About the same age as my Bianca, who's sleeping inside my camper."

"Bianca, I like that name. My daughter's name is Trudy. Short for Gertrude, named after her grandmother. Her food truck serves vegan food. It's difficult since her customers won't eat meat. They consider it cruel. She has to serve mostly plant food."

"Is she a vegan?"

"Goodness, no. But she's a sharp businesswoman like her father. Trendy sells. So, she'll cook trendy."

"Oh. Bianca does cupcakes. She makes the most beautiful wedding cakes using cupcakes. They're very elegant—with spun sugar and sugar sculptures. She's done lots of celebrity weddings. They've even appeared in food magazines."

"That sounds amazing. I love the Great British Baking Show.?"

"Me, too. Sounds like Trudy and Bianca would get along. My daughter doesn't make a move without a plan. Of my five kids, she's the most driven."

"Five. Catholic?"

"No. Jewish."

"I just have Trudy." With that, Trixie burst into tears again. "Oh, Mabel. This is all too much for me. First losing Ted. Then seeing ghosts—even though Ted did send Irma to comfort me. And not being able to find out exactly what happened to Ted."

"I know. I spoke to Ted. I was planning to come and see you. He wants you to stop. To just leave it alone and get on with your life. I'm sure he's tried to tell you.?"

"Yes, I know. Every morning when we have coffee together—I feel his presence, I hear his voice…" she took a gulp of water. "You saw him? He's handsome, isn't he?"

"Yes, he is. And he loves you very much. He wants you to live a happy life."

At that moment, Irma appeared. "Hello, ladies."

She was wearing a plum beaded sequin flapper dress and matching headband. Instead of feathers, she had a string of long pearls. Her hair was the iconic curled bob.

"Where's your hair?"

Irma looked at me with that — move along-nothing to see here—look.

"I know why you're here," Trixie said. "Irma, why can I see you and not my Ted?"

Irma walked very close to Trixie. "He's afraid if you saw him, it would magnify your grief. So, he just comes to you telepathically."

Trixie closed her eyes and nodded her head. "He's right. The grief is so dark. Just the same, the murderer needs to be brought to justice. The police are at a dead end. They think it was one of his mob clients. He's had lots of mob clients over the years. It wasn't anyone in the mob. I'm pretty sure I know who killed him."

Trixie looked at Irma and me and then said, "Cartel."

"Oh, that's bad," Irma said. "That's why Ted wants you to stand down."

"A member of the cartel hired Ted. He was a referral from a former mob client. He suspected his wife was keeping company with his brother. Another cartel drug lord. He wanted proof."

The wife showed up one day at Ted's office and begged him not to tell her husband. Told him she was ending the affair. That night, he sat me down to tell me about the visit. He wanted me to know just in case something happened to him. He said he had a bad feeling—like a premonition. We had an argument about taking on cartels as clients. He was leaving for Mexico the next day to deliver the proof to the husband. On his way to the airport, they were ambushed. He was shot and killed, as well as the driver. His briefcase was stolen. It had pictures. I know it had to be the brother who murdered Ted."

"How do you know for sure? You said yourself that Ted took on shady clients."

"The mob client who made the referral of the drug lord to Ted paid me a visit. It wasn't exactly a friendly visit. He warned me to stop looking into Ted's shooting —for my good — is the way he put it."

"I'm so sorry, Trixie, but I think you need to leave this alone. That guy who paid you a visit was giving you a clear warning."

"I know, but there is something I need to tell you. Which is the reason why I'm here. He had a message for you, Mabel."

"Me? What!!!"

"He told me to tell you that Lili needs to fall on the sword. Said you would know what he meant. It was for her own good and for her husband, Bob."

I saw the door to the camper open, and Bianca stepped out. She walked over in her Minnie Mouse PJs I had given her last Christmas. I remember they were too big when I sent them, but she was growing into them. She and my next grandchild.

"Bianca, this is Trixie. Her husband was Ted. He was murdered. He's spending time in purgatory with Irma, the ghost in my camper."

"Hello, dear," Trixie stood up and took Bianca's hand. "Your mother was just telling me all about you. You need to meet my daughter, Trudy. She has a vegan food truck. Sounds like you both have a lot in common. Here, sit down. I understand you are expecting."

Bianca sat down, and I grabbed another lawn chair.

"Mom."

"Yes. Are you okay?"

"I'm feeling just fine, but who is that woman over there dressed in a flapper outfit?"

I looked at Irma, who was waving at Bianca and blowing her kisses.

My jaw opened and closed. There were lightning bugs all around, and I didn't want to swallow one. I let out a loud sigh.

"That's Irma. I guess you got *I can see dead people genes* after all."

Chapter 16

"Excuse me," I said.

I got up, went into my camper to grab a bottle of water for Bianca, and poured myself a stiff shot of Kahlua, which I knew I would regret in the morning, and returned.

Irma had disappeared or was incognito, as she was from time to time.

"Bianca, can we talk a little later about Irma?"

"It's fine, Mom. She came over and introduced herself."

"You seem very calm about the fact that you can see spooks."

"I guess I am. Maybe it's the mountain air."

"Right."

"Mom. Your camper window was open, and I heard you and Trixie. That's why I got up and came out. I think the mob guy who paid Trixie a visit is the one who was sitting at the blackjack table with Aunt Lili. The one who shot Harold. Why else would he ask Trixie to deliver that message to you?"

I looked at my daughter and thought about that. It made sense.

"I think you might be right. He wants Lili to take the fall. Figure she and Bob will disappear into witness protection, and the FBI won't use that as leverage to get him to talk and accept whatever deal they offer him."

Then I asked Trixie a very important question. Her answer might save me a trip to Fish Camp.

"Trixie, do you know the name of this mob guy who paid you the unfriendly visit?"

"I do. He made a point of telling me his name and that he was a former client of Ted's. His name is Boris Popov."

"Russian mob?"

"He has ties to both. I kept the books and managed my husband's office. I looked up his file after he left. I guess you could call him a hybrid mobster. He reaches across the aisle."

"Why don't we reach out to that US Marshal and ask him to visit," I said, looking at Bianca. "Find out a little more about Boris. I think you should do the inviting. He'll be over faster that way," I said with a wink.

Bianca looked at me with that look your kids give you and then let out a big yawn.

"He called and left a voice mail asking me to go out to lunch with him. I was thinking of accepting his invitation. I'll bring it up in the conversation."

* * *

Bianca and I slept in after our late-night visitor.

Trixie had perked up and hung around and wanted to socialize. It was past midnight when I politely asked her to leave.

We were outside the next morning having our coffee when Bob walked over with his cup of coffee.

"May I join you?"

"Of course," I said.

"Bianca, it's wonderful to see you again. You look as beautiful as ever, and congratulations."

"Thank you, Uncle Bob."

Bianca adopted Bob when he married Lili.

"I hope we didn't keep you up last night. We had a visitor," I said.

"No, but someone banged on my camper door, and when I answered, she said she was looking for Mabel Gold. I sent her over to your camper."

"Well, she came over and banged on my door. Her name is Trixie. Her husband Ted was a private investigator, and he didn't discriminate with clients—mob and even cartels. He was shot and killed, and his briefcase was stolen. It contained proof that the wife of a cartel drug lord was having an affair with his brother, another cartel drug lord. He was on his way to Mexico to turn over the evidence. Pictures."

"Sounds like he got in the middle of something," Bob said.

I took a sip of coffee and a deep breath and said, "Bob, brace yourself for this."

Bob took a sip of his coffee and said, "Mabel, I'm a Marine, Special Forces, a homicide detective from LA, and I've met Lili's twin Jolene. I'm familiar with that term. Fire away."

"Trixie told us a former mob client referred the cartel guy to Ted. Trixie's pretty sure it was the brother who shot Ted and has been doing some snooping of her own to prove it. The police have reached a dead end. Recently, that mob guy paid a visit to Trixie. He told her to stand down."

"I hope she has," Bob said. "For her own good."

"Wait, there's more."

Bob was now giving me the steely look I knew he employed in the Marines.

"He also had a message for me."

"He had a message for you. A mob guy?"

"Yep."

Bob's jaw tightened. I could imagine young recruits shaking in their boots if he looked at them with that look.

"The message is for Lili."

"Mabel, I'm older now and can only take so much bracing. I've got a bad back."

"He said Lili should take the fall for the murder."

"Is he nuts! What's his name? This messenger."

"Boris Popov. That's what Trixie told us. He's Russian but works both sides of the aisle, according to Trixie. What do you think?"

Bob sat there a moment, finished his coffee, and got up.

"Ladies. I've got some things to do."

"Uncle Bob, I think he's the same mobster who was sitting at the table with Aunt Lili and shot Harold. Now he wants Aunt Lili to fall on the sword."

Bob turned around.

"What he wants and what he's going to get are two different things." Without another word, he turned and headed to his camper. I noticed that his hands had become fists. Anyone who got in his way would be sorry.

Bianca gave me the what's up with that look.

"He knows who Boris is. Pretty sure he's about to wake up some very important people and light a fire under them. He's got forty years of connections, and he's going to pull out all the stops."

Bianca got up and headed over to Bob's camper.

"Where are you going?"

"I'm going to ask Uncle Bob how I can help. I want in on this. Whatever it takes to get Aunt Lili home so we can visit."

"Hold your horses, warrior princess. I've learned the hard way one must be patient, and by being patient, you will be rewarded with the answer you seek.

"Mom, what show have you been watching on Netflix?"

"All of them. Let's give Bob a little time. He'll come back and tell us his news. Trust me, he's not going to let Lili sit in jail much longer. Even if it's a 5-star suite."

* * *

A few hours later, we were on our way to the famous Stanley Hotel. Bianca and I rode with Bob, and Josh and Peggy drove their huge Suburban.

I had wanted to cancel the trip, but Bob said we

should go ahead. That wheels were in motion, and we shouldn't worry.

So, there we were on our way to a ghost tour. When we arrived, there were two ghosts waiting to take the tour with us—Irma and Ted. They waved.

Once we were all together, Peggy didn't waste any time and started right in with a history lesson about the infamous Stanley Hotel. This time, she didn't come with brochures to pass around. She was holding a large picture book.

"The Stanley Hotel in Estes Park is a 142-room colonial revival hotel nestled in the Rocky Mountains. Here are the facts we should know about this hotel," Peggy said, as excited as a schoolgirl.

"Number one: Why is the Stanley Hotel so famous?"

Peggy looked at Bob and me and Bianca for an answer.

"It's haunted," Bianca said.

"That's correct, dear." Peggy smiled, and I noticed she was wearing lipstick and eye shadow and good golly, miss molly—false eyelashes.

"The Stanley Hotel is best known for being the inspiration for Stephen King's bestselling novel The Shining and the subsequent film starring Jack Nicholson as the slowly driven mad overseer."

"Do you know why Stephen King was inspired to write The Shining?"

I looked at Bianca, who was smiling at Peggy. She was enjoying this.

"Stephen King was inspired to write the book because of a nightmare he had at the hotel when he and his wife spent a night in room 217, to be exact. Mr. King woke up sweating all over. By the time he got up and finished a cigarette, he had the entire premise of the book mapped out in his head."

I looked over at two ghosts who were listening to the lesson. One was tapping her foot. That was not a good sign. Peggy continued, "Every single room in the hotel has experienced a spooky event. Clothes being mysteriously unpacked, lights going on and off, and objects moving on their own."

Peggy snapped the book closed—her signal that the lesson was ending.

"The Stanley Hotel employees assure guests that their ghosts are *happy* ghosts."

Bianca gave Peggy a round of applause. I looked over at the ghost still tapping away, and she said, "Yeah, sure."

Irma had previously told me she wasn't stepping foot in the Stanley Hotel. I was curious as to why she changed her mind. Trixie appeared and joined us at the end of Peggy's lesson.

"Trixie," I said.

"Thank you so much for inviting me."

Bob spoke up. "I reached out to Trixie and invited her to join us."

Right, I thought. Bob had something up his sleeve, and it probably had something to do with what Trixie shared with us. We spent the next hour touring the famous hotel. The walking tour gave us an opportunity to experience the hotel's history, architecture, and folklore. Our guide was a great storyteller. Ted was beaming, following along next to Trixie.

On the way out, I discreetly asked Irma.

"Why were you so adamant about not setting foot inside the Stanley Hotel? What made you change your mind?"

"Ted wanted to come along."

"Oh really. Is that the only reason?"

Irma puckered her face so tight I thought a few wrinkles were going to pop out. I was about to tell her not to hold her breath, but by then, that ship had sailed.

"I was afraid I was going to run into Walt's father. That's why."

"Oh," I said.

With that, she zipped off.

Irma had never spoken about that, but here it was. I may have to borrow that book from Peggy and read more about the Stanley Hotel and its many ghosts.

Chapter 17

Next, we were going to visit Lili since her hotel was nearby. Bob invited Trixie to join us, and she agreed. He wanted her to meet Lili. I knew he wanted to talk about the message from Boris and tell Lili in person. Peggy and Josh returned to the campground.

We entered the hotel, went up the elevator, and followed Bob to Lili's room, still heavily guarded. Of course, Bianca caught all their eyes, but only briefly. After all, they were highly skilled. When we entered the room, we found Lili and Jolene playing backgammon.

Bob stopped. Next, Jolene and Bob greeted each other in their usual way, which signified a truce because they shared a bond called Lili.

"Bob."

"Jolene."

Bianca ran over and gave Lili a big hug.

"You are feeling okay, dear," Lili asked Bianca, who smiled. Jolene got up and also gave Bianca a hug.

Bob was next and then me. Bob introduced Trixie. Once we were all seated, Special Forces Bob took over.

"Trixie's husband, Ted, was a private investigator here in Estes Park. He was murdered. Trixie has reason to believe it was by the brother of a cartel client."

"Oh, I'm so sorry," Lili said.

"Yes, my condolences," Jolene followed.

"Thank you," Trixie said, and then she burst out in tears.

Lili ran over and grabbed a box of Kleenex and gave Trixie the box and a hug, and Jolene went over and gave Trixie a pat on her arm and a squeeze. "Here, here," Jolene said.

"I'm so sorry," Trixie said as she stopped sniffling and blew her nose.

Trixie recounted the story of Ted's murder and then looked at Bob, who gave her a nod, and she told Lili and Jolene the message from Boris Popov.

"Is that so?" Lili said after Trixie finished, and then Bianca spoke next.

"Aunt Lili, Walt, ah, the US Marshal who was here the day when I arrived has asked me out to lunch, and I said yes."

"Why that rascal," Lili said. "Not surprised. I saw the way he was looking at you."

"I plan to ask him about this Boris Popov."

"Well, you are in luck. Walt is coming by any minute now. He's going to be happy to see you, Bianca."

I was surprised to see Bianca's cheeks turn a slightly darker pink. Was she blushing? The mountain air was doing her good.

Just then, the door opened, and in walked Walt, who

stopped in his tracks and stumbled over his words when his eyes saw Bianca.

"Bianca," he said.

"Hi, Walt. We came by to visit Aunt Lili."

Walt took a minute to look over the room and regain his composure.

"Sir," he said to Bob, who then introduced Trixie.

"I just came by to check on Miss Lili."

"That's very nice," Bob said.

"We're glad you are here. We'd like to have Trixie tell you something we think you should know and see if you could shed some light on a message that was delivered to Trixie to be given to Lili."

"Oh," Walt said and then looked at Trixie. He continued to stand and waited for Trixie.

"My husband, Ted, was a private investigator here in Estes Park. He never shied from clients connected to the mob, and recently he opened his practice to the cartel."

It looked as if Trixie was going to burst out in tears again, but she took a minute to wipe her eyes with the Kleenex.

Trixie then told Walt what happened to Ted, the message she received from Boris Popov, and how he was connected to her husband's death.

"I see," Walt said, looking around the room, and then his eyes came to a halt. He was looking into Bianca's beautiful eyes. The look on her face said it all. She was looking at him, and she was desperately asking for some answers for her Aunt Lili. At that moment, he decided.

"What I'm about to tell you must stay in this room. My job's on the line here."

"Roger that, son," Bob said.

"Boris Popov was sitting at the blackjack table with Lili that night. Harold's testimony sent his brother to prison. Yes, he shot and killed Harold."

"Okay," I said, pointing at Lili. "Then will Lili be released soon?"

"We are keeping Lili here for now for her own protection, and based on what you just told me, I'm going to speak to the FBI since this is becoming more serious."

"What do you mean?" Bob asked. "How much more serious could it become? My wife has been arrested for a murder she did not commit. I understand the concern, but it's time they arrested the person who shot Harold and release my wife."

Walt was silent and looked at Lili.

"Bob," Lili said. "Walt here has been speaking to me about the possibility of going into witness protection. I have no desire to enter witness protection and have told Walt."

Bob's face turned very serious. He was sitting next to Lili, holding her hands in his.

"Walt, please tell us what is going on?"

"I shared with you that the FBI has their own plans for Boris Popov. The charges against Lili have been dropped. To be honest, there were no charges. Your wife was at the wrong place wrong time. The FBI spoke with local law enforcement and took over Harold's murder investigation. But until they have Popov in custody, it's not safe to release Lili."

eyes I had not seen since the day she opened a pop-up bakery. "Walt is stationed nearby in New Jersey.

"Is that so?" Then I had to ask. "Does he know?"

"Yes. I told him."

"And?"

"He went out and bought a pink and a blue blanket."

Oh, my heart be still, and he was Jewish to boot. I told her I'd start planning the baby shower when I returned to Boca Vista in the fall.

Finally, it was time to leave Estes Park. "On the Road Again" was playing as we left, and our caravan headed to our next stop in the beautiful Rocky Mountains. Right next to me was my friend Irma.

"Keep your eye on the road, Mabel."

"Yes, ma'am," I said with a grin.

She was wearing a new outfit I had not seen before. She looked like she was going scuba diving.

"What's with the scuba diving outfit?"

It was getting close to September, and we would head back to Florida before long.

"Do you know who is buried at Neptune Memorial Reef?"

I knew a little about the reef. Bianca had told me about it when she told me Julia Child, the famous chef, was interred there.

"Well, it's a unique spot not too far from Key Biscayne. It's an underwater cemetery. You can choose to make it your final resting place. It stretches 16 acres on the ocean floor and is designed as a home for sea life and a destination for divers. Is that why you're wearing the scuba diving outfit?"

I realized I did not know where Irma's final resting place was located.

"Something Ted told me. Let's just say it's a heads up."

"Eyes on the road, Mabel, eyes on the road."

"Fine," I said. "Just fine."

For now, Thor was still pointed toward the Rockies.

I wasn't ready to end my camping trip yet.

Might never be.

A Note to the Reader

Dear Reader,

Thank you for reading, and I hope you will check out my other books. I would be most grateful if you could spread the word. In addition, I hope you will take a minute or two to post an honest review on Amazon.

If you would like to chat, I would love to hear from you.

Please email me at author@ritamoreau.com.

Drop in and say hello at

www.ritamoreau.com

www.facebook.com/RitaMoreauAuthor

www.amazon.com/RRMoreau

Until next time,
Rita

Acknowledgments

Rita Moreau lives in Florida with her husband, George, who brags to everyone that he is the author's husband. Without his motivation, there would be no author. Last year he crossed the shore. The author lost the love of her life but knows in her heart he is still with her and now tells everyone in heaven he is the author's husband.

To PatZi Gil for her support and friendship, I am forever grateful.

Thank you, my Beta readers, Georgia Tawil and Barbara Ellis. They possess sharp eyes.

To my niece, Indya Gordon, for sharing her good eats and recipes.

To April Putzulu for the scrumptious Kahlua cake recipe.

To the Town of Indian Shores Library volunteers and in particular Alice Lawrence, who have supported me all during my writing journey.

Finally, I am very grateful to you, my readers. If my novels bring you a good laugh and a little time for you, then my job is done.

Lili's Good Eats

Kahlua Cake

Ingredients
Devil's Food Cake Mix
1 cup sour cream
1 cup Kahlua
¾ cup vegetable oil
1 cup chocolate chips
4 eggs

Instructions
Combine ingredients and pour into a Bundt Cake Pan. Lili usually sprays the pan with Bakers Joy. Bake for 55 minutes at 325°F.

Mabel shared this one with Lili. It is a hit with the book club gals back in Boca Vista.

Linguine with Tomatoes, Feta, Olives, and Lemon

Ingredients
2 tablespoons olive oil
2 to 3 cloves garlic, peeled and minced
3 large tomatoes, peeled, seeded, and chopped
1 tablespoon chopped fresh oregano or 1 teaspoon dried, crumbled
12 to 16 ounces linguine, cooked and drained
8 to 12 Greek or Italian black olives, pitted and quartered lengthwise
4 ounces feta cheese, coarsely crumbled
Juice of 1-2 lemons
Salt and pepper

Instructions
Heat large skillet over high heat until very hot. Reduce heat to medium and add olive oil. Add garlic and sauté about 10 seconds.

Stir in tomatoes and oregano and simmer 7 to 8 minutes.

Add hot drained linguine and toss to coat pasta thoroughly with sauce. Add olives, feta cheese, lemon juice and salt and pepper to taste. Toss just to combine.

Lili says to serve immediately.

Cinnamon Coffee Cake

Ingredients
1 cup oil
2 eggs beaten
1 tsp vanilla
1 cup milk
1 cup sugar
3 cups flour
3 tsp baking powder
1/2 tsp salt
1 1/2 cup brown sugar
2 tsp cinnamon
1/2 cup butter melted

Instructions
In a large mixing bowl. combine oil, eggs, vanilla and milk together. In a medium bowl, blend together sugar, flour, baking powder and salt. Combine egg mixture with flour mixture. Pour half the batter into a lightly greased 9x13 pan.

In a medium bowl, prepare streusel by combining brown sugar and cinnamon.

Sprinkle half of streusel on top of the batter. Top with remaining batter and then sprinkle the remaining streusel on top. Drizzle with melted butter.

Bake, uncovered at 350°F. for 25-30 minutes.

A campground favorite.

An Excerpt From Bribing Saint Anthony

Before I wrote the Ghost & Camper Series,
I wrote the Mary Catherine Mahoney Series.

Here is an excerpt from book one —
Bribing Saint Anthony

Chapter 1

On one side sat 'blue blood, born rich,' who would never have to worry about money. On the other side sat 'gold digger, married rich more than once,' and any offspring would never have to worry about money. Cha-Ching, cha-Ching.

Each of these women had enough dough to single-handedly put a dent in the country's deficit, not to mention keep my small tax office afloat and eliminate any fear I ever had of having to move in with my aunts. Of course, without cultivating the psychic abilities I've been told I may possess, I failed to see the word 'disaster' spelled out in all caps on their wrinkle-free foreheads. Aunt Sophia would have clearly read, "Stop. Witch's Forest. Proceed, and you are toast."

I didn't need the family fortune-telling cards to tell me that across from my desk, sitting regal and upright, was the Queen Mother of Boca Vista, Babbs La-Fleur. Sitting right next to her sat the darling of Fish Camp, Jennifer Stone, aka the Queen of Hoochie Mommas.

On the alpha side sat Babbs: blond hair, patrician face, thin to the bone and dressed in casual rich. Not blinked-up rich, subdued rich. The type of rich you recognize after years of working at the IRS or Neiman Marcus.

Sitting next to Babbs on what appeared to be the hot seat was Jennifer Stone. Jennifer was genetically gifted by heaven at birth. Not with wealth, but with the other assets that would enable her to acquire all the wealth she would ever need, and then some.

Although Jennifer was not as rich as Babbs, but was a close second, thanks to a series of lucrative trophy wife marriages and the accumulation of the cash, alimony, and other assets acquired upon the dissolution of those marriages.

Jennifer, unlike Babbs, was not dressed in casual rich. She dressed in successful gold digger rich. Marilyn platinum blond hair piled high and teased in a throwback to the sixties beehive. She had the type of cleavage that could not be store bought and a figure way too petite for that cleavage, and jewelry, lots and lots of jewelry, expensive and flashy. No, there was nothing subtle about Jennifer Stone. She was, in a word, a Hoochie Mama. She loved NASCAR, honky-tonks and country music, and life in general, and karma returned the favor.

Queen Babbs came to life, took charge of the meeting and came right to the point.

"I understand you used to work for the IRS as an agent like my husband Charlie. In fact, you may have known my husband when he worked for the IRS in Fort Lauderdale."

"Yes. I remember your husband, Charlie," I said with my best professional smile.

Actually, I knew all about Charlie. He was a bit of a folk hero at the IRS. Charlie was a good man, but also a bad boy. Rumor was that he married Babbs for her money. Between husbands and wives, Charlie and I had a short fling. That was the extent of polite small talk while I felt myself blush red from the memory.

"My husband, Charlie has disappeared," Babbs said. I listened while she paused to watch my reaction. Gathering from the look on my red face, she registered that this was news to me and she continued. I glanced at Jennifer, who was busy admiring the rock on her manicured finger. No help there.

Babbs got out of the chair and walked behind Jennifer, who, on cue, looked up from the rock.

"He left right after the tax season ended," Babbs said, both women now looking straight at me.

At that point, the professional smile faded, and I got an uneasy feeling that something else was going on here, and it was being orchestrated by these two women. I looked up and saw Velma, out of the corner of my eye, standing by my office door eavesdropping.

"Go on," I said to Babbs as I looked away from Velma and flashed a weak smile. Jennifer went back to her rock admiration. Babbs stood behind her chair and continued with the story.

"Charlie usually takes off for his annual fishing trip to the Keys to celebrate the end of tax season. He is usually gone for about a week or two, and it's not unusual if I don't hear from him until he is heading back. When one week went by and then another, and I still had not heard from him, I started to worry," Babbs said while glancing over at Jennifer, who looked as if she had stopped breathing momentarily.

"Through information I had got through a contact, I had Bruce, my personal assistant, contact Jennifer and determine if she had any information related to his whereabouts," Babbs said while my brain was working to keep up and process this information. She then looked directly at Jennifer, who immediately looked up at me while placing her hands on her lap. The rock probably was getting heavy.

"What you may or may not know is that Charlie and Jennifer were having an affair," she said without blinking.

Jennifer looked up and took a deep breath and said, "Ms. La-Fleur, that is nothing but pure fantasy dreamed up by Bruce. I've told you before, and I'll tell you again, Charlie is my CPA, and that is the extent of our relationship. Bruce needs to stop playing the drama queen and inventing gossip."

Bruce was the Queen's personal assistant by title, pretty much Babbs's everything else. He was her chauffeur, her bodyguard, her food tester, her appointment handler, her personal shopper, and when needed, he even managed crowd control. He was her closest confidant.

Babbs shot her a queenly and authoritative look, which was basically the evil eye, which Jennifer returned in kind. Babbs ignored Jennifer's protests and directed her attention back to me, waiting for a response.

Wisely, I didn't say a word and was only wondering why we were having this gabfest in my office. It seemed more suited over a glass of wine at the local watering hole, and not my small tax and accounting office. I shot a quick sideways glance at Jennifer when Babbs took a minute to blink her eyelashes. Jennifer just looked at me with a blank slate on her face, giving me no clue. Out of the corner of my eye, I could see Velma, still at the door eavesdropping.

"The specifics of the affair are immaterial," Babbs said, as if she was dismissing and filing that report away. "I suspected it, and although I did not condone it, I accepted it. After all, I am several years older than Charlie," Babbs said with another batting of the eyelashes.

Out of the corner of my eye, I caught Jennifer rolling her eyes so far back that for a split second I thought I was going to have to get Velma to call 911. When I glanced at her, the blank slate was back.

"When Bruce and Jennifer talked, she told him she had not heard from Charlie either and was also worried about him," Babbs said. We both looked over at Jennifer, who continued to admire the rock that she had moved to the other well-manicured hand.

Jennifer sensed the stare and looked up and said, "Yes, that's correct," as if on cue but still eyeballing the rock, and then she added, "the part about not hearing from Charlie, but not the affair. Bruce, the drama queen, got that part right," she said, giving the rock a rest while looking straight at me.

Babbs just stared at Jennifer, let out a long sigh, shook her head as if dealing with a problem daughter, and then turned her attention back to me.

"Ms. Mahoney, I will get right to the point. I would like you to find Charlie," and then with real emotion, she added, "I don't care what he has done. Just tell him to come home, and all is forgiven."

I noted that Babbs said 'I would like you' as if giving me a direct order, as opposed to the normal 'I would like to hire you' I usually hear from my clients. The Queen thing. It was now my turn to speak. Those two were all of a sudden quiet and were both staring at me. It was a little unsettling and reminded me a bit of some of the family meetings I've had in the past with my mother and aunts. Jennifer had even stopped with the adoration of the rock on her finger and was giving me her undivided attention, once again, almost as if on cue.

"Ladies, to begin with, please call me Mary Catherine or MC for short," I said to them.

"Ms. La-Fleur, you seem a little confused. The services that I offer are accounting and tax related." And then I added, "It sounds like what you really need is a private detective." Fishing for a clue as to what was really going on here, I added, "If you do not want to report this to the police."

"Call me Babbs, dear," she said, and then waited for my response. "You, too," she directed the command to

Jennifer, who smiled back and silently mouthed "Okay."

I then stuck my foot in my mouth. "I have done some investigative accounting, but—"

"That is why I am here, MC," she said, now on a first name basis as she rose regally out of the seat and reached across the desk and patted my hand. I immediately sensed those two had set me up and were waiting for those words to open the door.

"I am aware of your reputation with the IRS as an investigative accountant. I think your job title was a Strike Force Agent," she said as she pointed her finger at me, not unlike my mother used to do… scary.

"I have been told that for investigative accounting, you were the best at the IRS." Babbs was now walking over to the window while I sat trying to get my foot out of my mouth.

I watched her and then I saw what caught her eye. It was Izzy, sitting on the window ledge looking back at her with his sweet, little iguana smile.

"What an unusual creature," Babbs said when she reached the window. "Personally, I feel sorry for the plight of the iguanas and do not condone the town's zeal to eliminate their population. I'll make a note to follow up with Bruce on this issue," she said regally.

I walked over and smiled at Babbs, and I tapped on the window with my 'get the heck out of here' look, but Izzy stood his ground. *Great. Now, I'm going to have to talk to Velma about Izzy.*

I smiled at Babbs again, gave Izzy a quick sneer, and went back to my desk. I guessed Charlie had told Babbs about my job at the IRS as a Strike Force Agent and my skills as an investigative accountant. Granted, the desperate housewives in town had discovered that I could track down their husband's hidden assets, but this woman knew something more than that about me and my work at the IRS.

"That's why I came to you," Babbs said, smiling back at Izzy and making her way back to her chair.

"I was told by good sources that if anybody could find Charlie, it would be you. That you could find Charlie exactly the same way the IRS got Al Capone."

Great, the barn door is wide open, and the animals are out. I just sat there in a pile of manure while she continued.

"I am prepared to give you access to all our financial records, bank accounts, credit cards, tax returns, etc. You can use those to trace my husband's whereabouts. Keep looking through those books and records until you locate him." Babbs paused for a second and added, "I tried a detective, but... let's just say it did not work out."

Babbs was now standing behind Jennifer, and they were both staring at me while I stalled to gather my thoughts. It was a little disconcerting. These two women were staring at me like cats waiting for the prey (me) to make a move. *Who in the heck had referred Babbs to me?*

"Okay, okay," I heard myself saying and stalling as best as I could. "So, you want me to go through your financial records to track Charlie down and determine his whereabouts?"

"Yesss," Babbs said, stretching out the "s" while arching her eyebrows, which were strangely not moving upwards. Jennifer was sitting upright in front of her, smiling back, and the beehive had started to bounce up and down. I expected bees to fly out at any moment. Taken off guard by the eyebrows and the bee hive, Babbs jumped in before I could say anything and said, "I always kept detailed records, even before I married Charlie." Of course she did, I thought. This woman was no dummy.

"In fact, I've kept up my personal financial records even after our marriage. Charlie assisted my Uncle Sal with the business since our marriage and also maintained his tax practice. I met Charlie when looking for a CPA firm for the business. Until then, running the family grocery business and everything that went along with that had been done by my Uncle Sal. But, he is getting older and not in the best of health," Babbs said.

"He kept his tax business records separate, but I have access to those, also, if you need them." And then she added, "I have a key to his office and can arrange for Bruce to take you there." She then wrapped up the speech.

"MC, you will have whatever you need at your disposal to find Charlie, whatever it takes. Whatever I own, consider it yours. I just want Charlie found and brought home," Babbs said to me and to Jennifer, who was now taking on the role of the dutiful daughter. Jennifer nodded at Babbs and flashed me one of her movie star smiles.

I was now sitting there in a full-blown hot flash. This
had nothing to do with taxes and accounting. Glancing
over at Jennifer, I suspected she was more involved
than she was letting on. Velma had slipped out and gone
back up front.

I said with little conviction, "Well, I don't know.
Like I said, it's really a job for a private detective and,
possibly the police."

At that moment Babbs, still standing behind her,
tapped Jennifer on the shoulder and said, "Jennifer,"
and pointed at her purse.

Jennifer, on cue, reached down and handed Babbs
her very expensive Prada purse. A purse that I knew
cost more than the entire wardrobe sitting in my closet.
Babbs opened the purse and took out a stack of cash
about an inch high and handed it to Jennifer, who
seemed, by instinct, to know what to do with cash. She
placed it neatly in the middle of my desk.

Silent once again, these two women were staring at
me, watching for my reaction. *Cash.* I was mesmerized
by it sitting squarely in the middle of my desk, an imag-
inary line between these two women and me. I knew if I
picked it up, I would cross over the line to the other
side and whatever these two had waiting for me. This is
where the Witch's Forest sign blinked like a neon sign.

"Ten thousand dollars," Babbs said and added, "just
to take the case, a retainer."

I sat there without moving or saying anything. CPAs
are not used to such big retainers. That kind of money
belonged to the high-powered, sleazy attorneys in the
criminal tax world.

Babbs tapped Jennifer's shoulder again and pointed to the magical purse. I watched as Jennifer pulled out an even larger stack of cash and lined it up next to the stack sitting in the middle of my desk.

"Would five thousand dollars a week plus expenses do?" Babbs looked at me as if she was negotiating re-decorating a vacation home, and then she added the closer.

"Whatever is mine is yours, my planes, cars, home and my entire staff."

I sat there in disbelief. The little voice in my brain was shouting at me by now, trying to tell me that this was more than a woman looking for a husband who had been gone a little longer than usual. But the cash on my desk was mesmerizing.

The office was still. Babbs had sat down, and both women were waiting across from my desk for an an-swer. They were staring at me like we were playing a game of poker, and by the looks on their perfect faces, they knew they had the winning hand.

By now, I wasn't watching the Witch's Forest sign or listening to the little voice in my head because all I could hear was the deafening sound of cha-Ching... cha-Ching. No worries for a while about paying bills, and best of all, no fear of having to move in with Aunt Sophia and Aunt Anna. I was hooked.

As I took a breath, Babbs, as if reading my mind, said, "Draw up the engagement letter and bring it to my house tomorrow. I will have Bruce call today to set up a time and go over any details. We will get you all set up in an office to go over the records." And with that, she reached over again and tapped my hand as if to say, "Don't worry, dear, it will be all right."

My brain was working at warp speed as they both got up to leave. Oh brother. I knew the cash was the lure that hooked me, but I also knew that I was also just plain curious about what was up with Charlie, and what was really behind this search for him by these two women. Curiosity had always been my weakness, and, it was what had made me so good at investigative accounting when I worked at the IRS.

"Well, I guess I could look into it," I said as I tried to muster some professionalism back into the meeting.

What harm could come out of it? It's amazing how the rationalization process kicks in as soon as you know you've made the wrong decision.

I was already working the plan out. I would look at the books and records, put my best investigative accounting to work, and get a lead on Charlie, who was probably down in the islands sipping rum. Then I would set up a meeting with the PI Babbs had hired. The PI could take it from there, pick up the trail, track down Charlie in no time, and have him home by dinner on one of those private planes. I could just picture that homecoming.

They were now quickly making their way out of the office. Jennifer stood, held the door and waited for Queen Babbs to exit, again playing the role of the dutiful daughter, when I woke up and said, "I will need the name of the private investigator you hired so I can arrange a meeting."

Babbs turned and looked at me with the cool demeanor of one who was holding the winning cards and now was showing her hand. "His name was Harry West. But he was found dead," she said. "Shot. You may have read about it in the newspapers." With that, the Queen turned to Jennifer, shaking her head, and heaving one big sigh.

Jennifer handed her the magic purse and waited to follow. Jennifer turned back and looked at me with an expression on her face that said, "I'm sorry" and then followed Babbs out of my office.

"Dead?" I said. Both women turned back to look at me with an expression on their flawless faces and sly smiles that said, "Is there any other way?" *Snookered!*

I sat there, unable to move. I had taken the bait, hook, line and sinker, and had just been reeled into the boat by Captain Babbs and her First Mate, Jennifer. I was now oblivious to the cash sitting on my desk as I heard Babbs going out the front door and Jennifer exchanging a few words with Velma.

I got up, still in a daze, and walked out to the front office as Jennifer went out the door. Velma was just sitting there, waiting to see the grand exit. We both walked to the window and watched as Bruce, wearing his chauffeur's uniform and cap, closed the door of the big, old black Rolls for Babbs, clicked his heels and got behind the wheel and took off.

As soon as the Rolls left, we heard the roar of the Corvette engine fire up, watched the top roll down all on its own, and in a split second, there was a flash of red followed by blond hair flying in the wind.

Something told me that both women were now wearing contented smiles. Babbs, in the back of her Rolls, probably sipping champagne and eating bonbons, telling Bruce all about the meeting; and Jennifer, with her radio blaring, singing along to country music, as she flew down the road.

To make matters worse, Izzy had slipped in through the front door and was now making his way to his perch on top of one of the filing cabinets in a closet I had converted for files when I had set up the office. I turned to Velma as I started back into my office and said, "You know, we really have to do something about that iguana."

She ignored me, following me into my office, but stopped cold and looked at the cash sitting on my desk.

"Whoa, I didn't know those fancy purses came with cash, too," she said.

"Neither did I," I said as we both stared at the cash like it was going to sit up and start talking to us.

"How much?" Velma asked.

"Ten thousand and change," I heard myself saying.

"I'd say it's more like twenty thousand," Velma replied.

"Really?" I said, looking up at Velma and then back at the two wads of cash sitting on my desk.

"Um hum," Velma said.

"There's only one way to find out for sure," and with that Velma reached down and grabbed a wad and started counting the cash.

"Lock the front door," she said not looking up at me.

I went up front to lock the door and turned to see Izzy behind me, heading into my office. I walked up, stopped in front of him, looked down and said, "stay." He looked up at me and, hearing the tone in my voice, turned around and headed back to his perch.

"Good boy," Velma said without turning around as I went back in and watched her pick up the second stack and finish counting.

"Finally," I said, "how much?"

Velma now had that smile on her face that she usually reserved for her favorite cheesecake.

"Twenty-five thousand," Velma said.

"You need to get this to the bank," Velma said as we went up front for something to carry the cash in, and then came back to scoop the bills into plastic bags from Walmart. "After that, we can talk about your meeting with the Queen."

I came back to life, grabbed my dusty gym bag sitting in the corner, and, after spilling its contents on the floor, stuffed the Walmart bags into it. I felt an urgency to get this much cash to a safe place.

"Ok, I'm going," I said to Velma as I stood there with my gym bag like I was heading for a workout.

"We will also talk again about that raise," Velma added. She definitely had that cheesecake smile on her face.

"After the bank, I have to go talk to Ernie and try to get a handle on this," I said as I made my way out of the office.

"Ernie? Are you nuts?" Velma said following me. "You're a CPA, not a spook, and Ernie is a spooky spook."

"Well, he's not really a spook. He worked for Homeland Security," I said.

"Homeland Security is the black hole for spooks. Trust me, that man was and *is* a spook," Velma said.

I thought about this for a minute while Velma headed out of my office to unlock the front door.

Velma had been privy to a lot of stuff in her position in Marathon, and before that, in the IRS office we worked at in Fort Lauderdale, where I had honed my investigative accounting skills. But where did she get a handle on how much cash was sitting on my desk? I put that thought on hold and opened the door to leave.

"Yeah, okay, I know, but it looks like folks around here think that since I worked for the IRS, and since CIA, FBI, and IRS are all three-letter words, that the jobs are synonymous. Anyway, I have a funny feeling he was the one who referred Babbs to me in the first place. Otherwise, how would she have known about my investigative background with the IRS? I want to find out why and what he knows about this PI of hers that was found shot dead."

So, I went out the door and headed to the bank with the dough. I looked back to see Velma waving goodbye, and Izzy sitting right there next to her as Velma closed the door. Snap!

Made in the USA
Las Vegas, NV
27 January 2024

85006792R00085